BEST SELLER ROMANCE

A chance to read and collect some of the best-loved novels from Mills & Boon—the world's largest publisher of romantic fiction.

Every month, four titles by favourite Mills & Boon authors will be re-published in the *Best Seller Romance* series.

A list of other titles in the *Best Seller Romance* series can be found at the end of this book.

Charlotte Lamb
DUEL OF DESIRE

MILLS & BOON LIMITED
15–16 BROOK'S MEWS
LONDON W1A 1DR

All the characters in this book have no existence outside the imagination of the Author, and have no relation whatsoever to anyone bearing the same name or names. They are not even distantly inspired by any individual known or unknown to the Author, and all the incidents are pure invention.

The text of this publication or any part thereof may not be reproduced or transmitted in any form or by any means, electronic, or mechanical, including photocopying, recording, storage in an information retrieval system, or otherwise, without the written permission of the publisher.

This book is sold subject to the condition that it shall not, by way of trade or otherwise, be lent, resold, hired out or otherwise circulated without the prior consent of the publisher in any form of binding or cover other than that in which it is published and without a similar condition including this condition being imposed on the subsequent purchaser.

*First published in Great Britain 1978
by Mills & Boon Limited*

© Charlotte Lamb 1978

*Australian copyright 1978
Philippine copyright 1979
This edition 1984*

ISBN 0 263 74925 8

*Set in Linotype Baskerville 10 on 11 pt.
02–1084*

*Made and printed in Great Britain by
Richard Clay (The Chaucer Press) Ltd,
Bungay, Suffolk*

CHAPTER ONE

APRIL was ending, as it had begun, with showers that came without warning from a clear blue sky, and people carried umbrellas under their arms in precaution, opening them hurriedly as rain splattered suddenly and a dark cloud passed overhead. Deborah had paused to admire the windowboxes of the bank, gay with scarlet tulips whose waxen petals and bright colours were almost artificial in their regularity. Now she hurried on, quickening her steps towards the plate-glass exterior of her office block two doors away. The pavements were thronged with people. Sleek limousines edged their way along between dark strings of taxis who, for all their bulk, manoeuvred briskly in and out of the traffic jam which was building up. Bond Street lay just around the corner and at nine-thirty on a weekday morning the streets of this part of London were crowded.

As Deborah approached the commissionaire saluted, his white-gloved hand rising smartly in a military movement, his dark uniform enriched with gold braid. Wealthy companies inhabited the tall block behind him, and security was tight. He knew most of the employees who worked there by sight, some of them by name. The electronically controlled doors were operated from the foyer by a young woman seated at a desk. Deborah moved forward as there was a buzz and the doors slid open.

'Terrible weather, Miss Portman,' the girl said chattily, without bothering to glance at Deborah's proffered security pass.

'Let's hope it will clear before lunch,' said Deborah, walking towards the lift.

She had worked there since leaving school and was well known by sight. The receptionist watched her enviously. Deborah Portman's job required that she look elegant, and the other girl wondered how she contrived to make a simple black dress look as if it had been made in Paris. Over it she wore a short black jacket which swung from her slender hips as she walked. Tall, for a girl, she had the fine-boned build of a model, her oval face framed in smooth ash-blonde hair, worn in classical purity, swathed in a smooth chignon. It was no wonder, the receptionist thought dreamily, that Alex St James had chosen her as his personal assistant. No doubt her looks had got her the job.

In the lift Deborah was thinking ahead to the work she had to get through. She frowned, remembering that Alex would be back from a flying visit to Stockholm. She always found it easier to work when he was absent. Emerging into a blue-carpeted corridor, her footsteps silenced by the depth of the pile, she passed steel-framed prints of eighteenth-century London life which familiarity had rendered invisible to her. She pushed open the heavy plate-glass doors which bore the name ST JAMES MUSIC printed on them in large gilt letters, passed through the small reception area, smiling at the young receptionist, and crossed into the open-plan office beyond. Half a dozen girls were typing at desks, their heads turning as she appeared. They smiled at her, chorussing a greeting, and she smiled back as she walked to the opaque-glass door which bore her own name.

The firm occupied the whole of the fifth floor. There were some dozen different offices leading off the open area. Her own boss, the managing director, had a large square room beyond her own, with a door communicating between them.

She had worked for Alex St James for four years now. For several years before that she had worked as a secretary before being promoted at the age of twenty-two, and she knew that her air of reserved efficiency had been responsible for her elevation. Working with temperamental musicians, Alex St James had looked for someone even-tempered with sufficient common sense to deal with the artistes.

Before leaving work the previous evening she had tidied her office, preferring to find it spick and span when she began work in the morning. She had a passion for orderliness. Now she stood, glancing around the room with eyes which missed nothing, before, satisfied, she hung her jacket on a coat-hanger, tucked away that maddening stray lock of hair which somehow always managed to escape her, then walked to her desk.

While she was glancing through the post the door opened and a voice barked at her, 'Come through!'

She put down the letters and walked into the other office. Alex was holding his green appointments book, a frown corrugating his brow. Deborah stood, her face expressionless, waiting.

He glanced up and a flicker of sardonic irritation crossed his face. 'Sit down,' he said sharply.

Alex St James had inherited an old-fashioned music company from his father ten years earlier, transforming it over the years into a dynamic modern firm which had gradually acquired a small, but hugely profitable, list of recording stars. His energy and intuition were indisputable—Deborah reluctantly conceded his flair. Professionally, she admired him. As a man, however, he aroused a strong hostility in her, a silent emotion of which he was well aware.

In his late thirties, built on lean but muscular lines, he tended to dress casually even for work, wearing expensive but figure-moulding shirts in dark colours, thrust into tightly-fitting denim pants, often worn with a matching jacket. He rarely wore a tie, often left his collars undone, and wore his thick black hair loose down to his collar in a style which Deborah considered untidy. His face was hard, energetic, sometimes full of charm, always disturbingly attractive. His eyes were a grey so light as to be silvery. In temper they took on the colour of steel and sparked with rage. His cheekbones were angular, fleshless, almost austere. His mouth was a little too wide, the top lip firm and controlled, the lower fuller, conveying the hint of sensuality. His face reflected his mood, sometimes cruel, sometimes scornful, always full of a personal instinctive power. He looked as though he ran on electricity. Sometimes he seemed almost incandescent, his mind revolving rapidly, so far ahead of her own that she resented his ability to think faster than normal humans.

The basis of her secret hostility towards him was her personal aversion to his code of living. He pursued success with grim intensity. He worked and played hard. He used his undoubted sex appeal mercilessly. His name had been coupled with a succession of stars. She often suspected Alex knew how to manipulate the media too well—a new star often got acres of free publicity by being seen night-clubbing with him for a few weeks. The restaurant gossip saved the firm a fortune spent on publicity. These relationships fizzled out rapidly, for one reason or another. He showed no signs of marrying, and none of his affairs had ever appeared serious. His ruthless attitude appalled her.

When she first began to work for him he had several times asked her to dine with him, but she had politely but firmly refused all invitations. His response had been a needling form of mockery. Her cool good looks and quiet manner had infuriated him. She had ignored his constant barbed remarks, maintaining her own temper with difficulty, then one day had lost her temper and snapped back at him. His amusement had softened their relationship, and for a brief time they had worked together in comparative harmony. Suddenly Alex had asked her out again, but quietly she had told him that she was already engaged for the evening. His narrow-eyed surprise had amused her. He had not believed her excuse until he discovered that she was regularly dating the firm's accountant, Robin Mayhew. Deborah had been seeing Robin for some months. Her working relationship with Alex had become barbed again, and she was always relieved when he was away on business. When it was necessary for her to accompany him on his trips abroad she found the experience unnerving. When she was alone with Alex she always felt her nerves prickling uneasily. He was as difficult to handle as a wild eagle; savage, unpredictable, predatory.

'How many of my appointments for tomorrow and Friday would you say were urgent?' he asked her suddenly, catching her staring at him.

She flushed at his narrowing eyes. He was conceited enough to imagine all the wrong reasons for her gaze. Aloud she said quietly, 'Only the one with Sammy Starr. Her contract is up for renewal.' She lowered her lids, adding remotely, 'And you have a lunch date with Miss Gilmore tomorrow.' Magda Gilmore was a bronze-haired model whom he had been seeing a good deal recently. Working for one of the new, smaller fashion houses, her barbaric hair-style and outlandish style of dress were more than offset by her exquisite figure and beautiful face. Her high cheekbones sometimes had a hectic flush. She laughed excitedly, in flute-light tones. She had the in-face of the moment. Deborah saw her face on magazines and in television advertisements. Alex always went out with girls whose appearance created public interest. His nose for public relations was impeccable and he preferred free publicity to paying for it.

He was smiling reminiscently when she looked up. 'Ah, yes,' he said softly. 'Magda . . .' He sat down on the edge of his desk, his lean thigh pressing against her own. Deborah imperceptibly moved, and at once he looked at her derisively, bringing a flush to her cheek.

'We have to fly over to Nice,' he said. 'You'll have to cancel all our appointments until Monday. Try to get Sammy to come in and see me today if she's free. Is the contract ready?'

'Yes,' she said, her brow creasing. 'When you say we . . .'

He interrupted her with dry emphasis. 'I mean you and me, Miss Portman. This is one of those trips on which your presence is essential!'

He normally only took her with him when secrecy was essential. Secretary after secretary had proved to be indiscreet. Excitement or corruptibility had made them leak vital information before deals were signed, and Alex now refused to trust anyone but Deborah on such occasions.

She gave him a look of dismay. 'Have you forgotten? I have an important date this weekend. I mentioned it to you before you left for Stockholm. I can't be away.'

His mouth tightened. 'I'm sorry,' he said, 'you've got to be there. I shall need help on this one. Anyway, you can fly back on Friday evening. Your weekend won't be in any danger.'

She stared at him hesitantly. Nothing must interfere with the weekend trip; Robin would never forgive her. 'Couldn't you take Linda?' she asked. Linda Evans, the most senior of the secretaries, worked for Alex's second-in-command, Joe Cohen, and was aware of some of the more private business which Alex preferred to have dealt with by his own office.

'No, I can't,' Alex said decisively. The silvery eyes surveyed her grimly. 'What's so vital about this weekend? Are you going away with Robin?'

Something in his tone brought a flush of dark red into her face. Her eyes hardened. 'No,' she snapped. Then she hesitated, her logical mind reminding her that, in fact, she was doing just that, but not in the sense in which he had undoubtedly meant it. She added in very uncharacteristic confusion, 'That is ... well ...' Her flush deepened at his gaze. 'I'm going to stay with his family,' she said in defiance, her rounded chin lifting.

'My God!' he said mockingly. 'He's taking you home to meet mother, is he? I'm sure she'll approve of his choice. You have that sweet virginal look every mother wants for her son.'

Her eyes darkened with anger. 'I did tell you about it,' she said. 'I remember speaking to you.'

'I doubt if I heard a word,' he said, shrugging. 'I was too concerned with the Stockholm trip to listen to your romantic confidences. What difference does it make? We'll fly back on Friday in plenty of time for you to meet Robin. I've a pleasant weekend planned for myself, so we won't miss the plane.'

Deborah stared at him indecisively, the tip of her tongue worrying the centre of her lower lip.

The grey eyes dropped to her mouth and with a faint sensation of uneasiness she hurriedly closed her lips, looking away. It infuriated her that, despite her dislike of him, she should be unable to avoid an occasional awareness of him.

Sighing, she said, 'Very well. I'll make the reservations.'

His voice sounded abstractedly intent. 'Good,' he murmured. She looked up again and their eyes met. She felt a peculiar sensation run down her spine, as though he had touched her.

'I heard in Stockholm from a reliable source that Ricky Winter's contract with Wolf Music comes up for renewal soon and he's in the middle of a row with Russ Wolf. If I could sign him before anyone else gets to him it would be a feather in our caps.'

Her eyes widened. 'Ricky Winter... he's good.'

'Better than that,' Alex said scornfully. 'He's fantastic, but pretty difficult to handle, they say. It won't be easy to get him. I want to keep this under wraps until I've made the contact. Linda is a nice girl, but I can't afford to have the news leak out.'

'Linda is very discreet,' she said indignantly. Linda was a friend of hers, and she was certain she could be trusted.

'Don't fly off the handle,' he said. 'Ricky Winter is far too important for me to take any risks.'

She shrugged. 'Which hotel shall I book us into?'

'April is low season,' said Alex indifferently. 'Anywhere will do.'

Leaning over his desk, he scribbled down a number, his body swinging round so that again his legs brushed against hers, the lean muscles hard against her silk-clad calf. Deborah pulled back nervously and he straightened, his derisive glance informing her that he had noted her second withdrawal from physical contact. 'Ring Miss Gilmore at this number and tell her I have to cancel our date,' he said. 'I'll ring her when I get back from Nice.'

She rose, unavoidably coming closer. Their faces were inches apart, their eyes meeting with veiled expressions. Irritably she felt the powerful tug of Alex's sexual attraction. No woman working in such close proximity to an attractive male could be blind to his sensual appeal, and it was not the first time she had felt instinctively aware of him. The grey eyes held her glance for a second, then dropped to stare deliberately at her mouth, clearly conscious of the heat which came into her face. Although she had no strong feminist leanings, Deborah found it irritating that Alex should treat her less as a capable colleague than as a desirable woman, silently making it clear that he was aware of her sexuality. Far from being flattered she felt infuriated. His permanent involvement with other women made these moments insulting. They were the automatic gestures of a man who used his sex appeal ruthlessly, and she despised them.

Moving back into her own office, she first rang Sammy Starr, who answered after some time in a sleep-drugged voice and was raucous about having to come into London at such short notice. 'But I'll be there,' she added with a smile coming into her voice. 'If Alex whistles, who wouldn't run?'

Ringing off, Deborah made a face at the receiver. Alex had been very attentive to Sammy Starr when she first joined their list, but the relationship had imperceptibly cooled after a while, although she suspected Sammy still carried a torch for him. The five-foot high, rough-voiced Australian singer made no secret about her passion for him. Deborah had once seen her kiss him passionately at a large party, her arms flung round his neck in blatant ownership. Alex had seemed amused rather than embarrassed. His glance at Deborah a moment later had been wickedly sardonic. She had felt angry pity for the twenty-year-old Sammy, although Sammy's vital cheerfulness had not really demanded it. Deborah had never noticed any signs of bitter grief when Sammy visited them. She appeared to have accepted her loss of Alex with good humour.

She picked up the telephone again and began to make a list of phone calls, cancelling her appointments. Then she got on with her work, her face smoothing out into absorption as she became engrossed.

Alex called her into his office some hours later. He had taken off his jacket and was deep in paperwork, his desk awash with it. The collar of his shirt was open, and against his brown throat she saw a silver medallion Sammy had given him for luck after her first concert. He turned, his dark hair flicking back, and eyed her sardonically.

'You always look as if you were about to open a bazaar,' he said, the silvery eyes running down over her slender body, lingering on her long smooth legs.

'You look as if you've been dragged through a hedge backwards,' she retorted tartly.

He smiled. Deliberately he undid two more buttons on his shirt, revealing the fine dark hair on his muscular chest. 'It's warm for April,' he said casually, watching her.

'I'm going to lunch,' she said abruptly, on the point of going.

'Did you ring Miss Gilmore?' he asked, halting her.

'Yes. She asked if you could ring her yourself.' Her tone held nothing but polite indifference, although she had felt sorry for Magda, whose dismay at the news had been obvious.

'And you told her?' he asked.

'That you were busy but would try,' she said, her eyes on the changing sky.

'Soul of tact,' he murmured drily. 'You managed to make the Nice reservations?'

'Yes,' she agreed.

'Separate rooms, of course?' he asked in deliberately taunting tones which brought her averted gaze to his face in immediate anger.

'Yes,' she said tightly.

He leaned back in his chair, his fingers playing with

the silver medallion, the small movement unavoidably attracting her attention. 'When is the happy announcement to be made?' he asked softly. 'I presume you are getting engaged to Robin this weekend?'

'Yes,' she said flatly. 'At a party for his parents' wedding anniversary. Robin thought it would be a suitable occasion.'

'How very neat,' he said sardonically. 'The accountant's mind—balance the books. Keep neat columns. Economise, even on emotion.'

Deborah's face tightened with anger, but she firmly ignored his attempt to make her rise to his bait.

'I don't want to be late for lunch,' she said, glancing at her wristwatch.

The restless silvery eyes slid over her again. 'The two of you will suit admirably,' he said in barbed tones. 'You'll do the household accounts instead of making love and never let the emotional temperature rise above zero.'

Her eyes flashed in irritation. 'You're hardly in a position to criticise us,' she said, her temper suddenly flaring. 'What you know about marriage could be written on a postage stamp!'

'You talk about marriage,' he said tersely. 'What about love? You've been going out with Robin for months. It took long enough for you to make up your mind to marry him.'

'We were neither of us in a hurry,' she said angrily.

'Evidently,' he snapped. 'Have you been to bed with him yet?'

The question took her breath away. Feeling her face burn, she said bitterly, 'How dare you ask such a personal question?'

He was on his feet, a few inches away from her, before she was aware he had moved. Looking down at her fixedly, he said, 'I'm damned sure you haven't. A few kisses here and there are the extent of your experience. If I were you I would find out what sort of lover he is before I married him.'

'Your opinion isn't worth a row of beans,' she said furiously. 'Just because you leap into bed at the drop of a hat it doesn't make you an expert on love. If I marry Robin it will be because I know I'll be happy with him, not because I want to ...' she broke off, realising with horror the danger of finishing the remark.

His eyes narrowed on her flushed, dismayed face, and a gleam came into those silvery depths. 'Not because you want to sleep with him? Interesting, Miss Portman. Poor Robin! Does he know he's marrying an icicle? I wouldn't have said Robin was entirely sexless. It seems rather unfair to marry him feeling like that.'

Bitterness came in to the back of her throat. She looked at him, words boiling inside her head. 'You ... bastard!' Choked, humiliated, she could barely enunciate.

Alex smiled tigerishly, the full sensual lower lip quivering with amusement. 'My God, this is the first time I've ever seen the cool, unshakable Miss Portman lost for words! Did I hit a sensitive target?'

She looked at the mocking, smiling face with a hatred that brought a red mist before her eyes. Then her hand flew up, slapping him viciously across his face, her rage needing some outlet for the shame and frustrated anger which were burning inside her.

The smile vanished from his face. For a second he looked stunned, then slowly he touched the red mark across his cheek with a hand that held her gaze in hypnotised dismay.

Her action had released her tongue. Stammeringly, she said, 'I shouldn't have done that ...' She was horrified by the naked emotion she had displayed. She had never done such a thing in her life before. She detested scenes, and was appalled at having made one, even under the sting of his derision.

'You shouldn't,' he agreed grimly. He seized her hand and carried it inexorably to the place where it had struck earlier, opening the fingers until they lay against the red mark.

She quivered, feeling the warmth of his skin against hers. His eyes held her glance. 'A little higher and I would have had a black eye,' he told her. 'How would I have explained that?'

She attempted to pull her fingers out of his grip, but he held them firmly beneath his own, pressing them hard against his hot cheek.

'You provoked me,' she said anxiously, half in protest, half in dismay.

'You've been provoking me for four years,' he said softly.

Her eyes widened, then fell away. The quivering in her body grew. 'I've got to go to lunch,' she said weakly. 'I'm meeting Robin, and I'm late now.'

'Will you tell him you slapped my face?' he asked teasingly.

She silently shook her head.

'It would shock him beyond belief,' Alex said sardonically. 'Robin has a very orderly mind.'

'He respects you,' she said rebelliously. 'Do you think I could repeat the things you said?'

He laughed, unabashed. 'I've no doubt he would decide I'd only been teasing you. Robin has a convenient mind. It rationalises what it prefers not to see.'

Deborah looked at him, half irritated, half impressed. Robin's habit of ignoring what he preferred not to see had often angered her.

Alex slowly moved her hand from his cheek, still

imprisoning it. 'I suppose if I asked you to kiss it better, you'd refuse?' he asked, tongue in cheek.

'You suppose quite correctly,' she retorted.

His gaze focussed on her mouth disturbingly. 'Pity,' he said softly. 'Do you realise I've known you for four years and I've never kissed you?'

Hot-cheeked, she said huskily, 'I'm sorry to be your one failure.'

He smiled tantalisingly. 'Are you, Deb?'

The rare use of her christian name made her spine tingle with alarm. She backed, tugging at her imprisoned hand, but suddenly he jerked on it violently, pulling her forward. Brought up hard against his shirt, she pushed at his chest with her free hand, feeling the inflexible strength of the muscles under her palm, the animal warmth of his body striking into her own flesh. She had always avoided such close contact with him before, but the faint fragrance of his after-shave was familiar.

'Let me go,' she murmured angrily, but his free hand came round her, stroking the tense muscles of her back almost absently, while he watched her in unusual intensity.

'You don't even like to have me touch you, do you, Deb?' he asked curiously. 'You move away whenever I'm anywhere near you. Do all men affect you the same way?'

'No, just you,' she snapped, before realising the revelation behind her reply.

His eyes narrowed. 'Do you know, I suspected as much,' he said softly.

Her eyes fell before the penetration of his stare, and she said nervously, 'Robin will wonder where on earth I've got to ... let me go, Alex, please ...' then felt a sense almost of panic as she heard herself utter his christian name. She had known from the start that she must always keep the formality of surnames between them for her own self-protection, and her lapse sent a wave of alarm down her back.

He lazily moved a hand to the stray lock of hair which was curling down against her white temple, playing with it idly. 'You've always had one little curl loose, like the girl in the nursery rhyme ... the rest of you is as neat as a new pin. That wayward lock is revealing.'

She wriggled in the prison of his arms, her heart beating fast, but before she could frame another request to be freed, he suddenly bent his head and took her mouth softly, the slow sweetness seducing her lips apart, his hands sliding down her body in an intimate movement which made her head swim. Warmth flowed along her limbs wherever his hands touched. She gasped protestingly under his lips, and he lifted his head with a slow, reluctant movement.

They stared at each other in a silence in which she could hear the sound of his heart beating against her own. Huskily he said, 'I've wanted to do that for years.'

Her heart missed a beat. She found the darkened look in his eyes disturbing. With difficulty she made herself stiffen, pushing him away. 'I'm not putting up with being used as an amusement for your idle moments, Alex. I think you'd better have my resignation.'

For a moment he neither moved nor spoke. Then his hands fell away and he straightened, allowing her to stand alone.

Deborah felt her breathing slow to its normal rhythm, her heart beat calming. Anger and fear made her voice bitter, as she said, 'I'll leave today.'

'You can't,' he said abruptly. 'In your contract it stipulates three months' notice.'

'I'll forfeit my salary for that period,' she said immovably.

'I'll sue you,' he retorted.

'I don't give a damn!' she flung back, her eyes burning with hatred.

'Robin will care,' he said softly.

Her eyes spat contempt at him. 'Not when I tell him ...'

'That I kissed you?' His face mocked her. 'I would have to rape you for Robin to agree to forfeiting money.'

Her cheeks burst into dark red colour. Alex laughed at her, his hands thrust into his pockets.

'Anyway,' he said, shrugging, 'this is a storm in a teacup. What's a kiss after four years? It hardly constitutes a hanging offence. I need you on this Nice trip. Ricky Winter is hard to handle and you always manage to seduce difficult young men so sweetly.' He gave her an insolent smile. 'If it were a girl, I'd handle it myself.'

'I'm sure you would,' she said bitterly. 'Very expertly.'

His eyes mocked. 'Exactly. We'll scrub what happened I promise, I'll dance at your wedding with gentlemanly discretion.'

Deborah was torn between a reluctance to give up her job and a fear of the emotions which had flared between them just now. Working for Alex St James was a little like handling dynamite. One needed a cool head, and after the last few moments Deborah was no longer sure she could keep her head if he chose to make certain she lost it. She had always feared such an incident. Now she was confused and uncertain.

Alex was watching her keenly, observing the fleeting emotions in her blue eyes with shrewdness.

'I must resign,' she said slowly. 'All right, I won't

leave right away, but you must take three months' notice.'

He stared at her unreadably, his expression masked. Slowly he shrugged. 'As you like. You'll never get a job as good as this one again. You're good at it and you enjoy it. But if you want to cut your nose off to spite your face ...'

'I've never wanted to work after I'm married,' she said lightly. 'Robin and I want a family.'

Alex turned away and walked to the window, staring out at the sky, his shoulders tense. 'Go to lunch, Miss Portman,' he said curtly.

CHAPTER TWO

STILL very flushed, Deborah opened the door of Robin's office, three doors from her own, and glanced across the immaculately tidy room. Robin was at his desk, his head bent over an open file of papers. For a few seconds Deborah eyed the top of his head with affectionate but half irritated amusement. Then he looked up absently, met her glance and broke into a smile.

'Oh, no! Am I late for lunch? Darling, I'm terribly sorry...' He jumped up, crossed the room in two strides and kissed her warmly, his mouth gentle. 'You look beautiful,' he told her, admiring her new dress. 'Gorgeous enough to eat. I won't keep you a moment. Must just put that file away—you know how Alex is about security...' He drew a key from the small collection on the gold watch-chain he wore across his dark waistcoat and she watched as he carefully deposited the file into a drawer and locked it. He glanced over his desk briefly, smiled and turned towards her. 'Ready,' he said.

Robin was just thirty years old; a broad, well-built man whose clean-cut, rugged good looks did not go unadmired as they passed through the open office a moment later. Several of the younger girls fought over the honour of taking him coffee and doing work for him, although in a straight contest between the two men none of the girls were ever in any doubt that Alex was the more glamorous of the two. Robin had eyes and hair close to the colour of chestnuts in autumn, a rich, glowing brown enlivened by touches of gold. His features were regular, as well balanced as his calm nature; a strong, affectionate mouth, accustomed to smiling, a pleasantly shaped nose, a strong chin and broad, flat cheekbones which gave a Dutch placidity to his smile at times. He was not, Deborah knew by now, a passionate man, but his own secure, loving family background made him easy and confident in his way of meeting the world. Robin had taken their relationship in his stride, in no hurry to make decisions about the most important matter in his life, and Deborah had been sufficiently interested in her own career to accept without anxiety the unhurried pace of their courtship.

Deborah's parents had died in a fire during her first year of life. She had been found in her pram, in a garden under a sunny tree, some time later, crying pitifully. Her parents, having put her out into the garden on a Sunday morning after breakfast, had apparently intended to sleep for an hour, during which time the sitting-room had caught fire and, it was suspected, the young parents had been overcome by smoke. The only relative she had who was prepared to look after her had been an elderly uncle, Roger Seal, who had been sufficiently well-to-do to be able to pay for a nurse for her in her early years, and then, as soon as it was possible, had sent her off to boarding school. Her uncle had died during her final year at school, leaving enough money to finish her education. Deborah was grateful to him for the financial care he had taken of her, but the way in which she had been brought up had left her emotionally starved for affection, although she had learnt to be independent.

It had been Robin's nature which attracted her to him. He carried about with him such an air of unruffled warmth. He talked frequently of his family, his parents, two sisters and brother. Deborah loved to listen to his tales of family life, to his childhood reminiscences, his jokes and nostalgia, the whole fragrance of family which enclosed him. Domesticated, affectionate, Robin seemed to her the perfect husband. As a lonely child at boarding school she had always longed for just such a life, busy, energetic, loving. Robin's small idiosyncrasies never bothered her. She approved of his carefulness about money, his economies and neatness of mind. An accountant by profession, he had a nature that inclined him to balance everything before action, and he had brought the same care to his romance with Deborah.

They lunched at a small restaurant a block away. It was one of their accustomed haunts, and the waiter smiled at them as he came to take their order. Deborah, without needing to consider the menu, ordered minestrone soup followed by chicken salad. As the waiter moved away, Robin said with a smile, 'Looking forward to the weekend?'

Deborah's relaxed expression tightened. 'Very much,' she said quickly. 'But ...' she paused, biting her lower lip, 'Alex wants to take me to France with him tomorrow on a business trip.' She saw Robin frown, and added quickly, 'We'll be back on Friday night, so there's no danger that I'll miss the weekend.'

Robin's brows drew together. He fiddled with his cutlery, eyeing her silently. Then he said slowly, 'Refuse to go, Deb.'

Something in his voice surprised her. She looked at him anxiously. 'I did try to get out of it, but it's very secret—one of his big deals. I can't give you any of the details, but it's true that we can't afford news of it to leak out. There's no time to waste, so I can't even ask him to wait until after the weekend.'

Robin's face did not reflect resignation. Instead his brown eyes fastened on her face with a frown in them. Slowly, he said, 'I respect Alex. He's marvellous at his job. I admire the way he operates. But to be frank, my parents are concerned about your frequent trips abroad with him. He has a reputation, Deb.'

Her face flamed and her blue eyes widened. 'You can't suspect ...' Her voice broke off angrily and she swallowed. 'Robin, you've never given me a hint before that you were worried ... You must know that Alex and I are ... Good God, I've never been involved with him!'

He leaned across the table, taking her hand quickly. 'I know,' he said gently. 'I've made it quite clear to my ... my parents that I trust you, that there's nothing between you and Alex.' His face reflected uncertainty. 'To be absolutely frank, though, this is one reason why I delayed the announcement of our engagement.'

Deborah was taken aback, staring at him in indignant amazement. He had never, by a hint or word, given her any sign of jealousy. Indeed, he had always seemed to respect and admire Alex without hesitation. The waiter appeared before she could speak, placing her first course in front of her. When he had gone she said quietly, 'Why have you never said anything before, Robin?'

He shrugged. 'I told you, I've never given Mother's suspicions any credence. Good lord, I know you aren't sleeping with Alex!'

'Sleeping with him?' Her voice was stifled but husky with shock.

Robin looked unhappily at her. 'I know, it's ridiculous ... I've never suspected it for a moment.'

'Then why did you delay our engagement?' she asked point-blank, her voice stiff.

'To give Mother time to get used to the idea,' he said, a little uneasily. Confusion made his face flush. 'I put that badly ...' He gave her an embarrassed smile. 'I know she'll love you when she meets you. What I meant was ...'

'I'm beginning to see what you meant,' she said curtly. 'Robin, is that why you've never taken me down to see your family? I thought it was just because you wanted to be quite sure of the future before we made anything so formal as a family visit.'

'That's true,' he said quickly. 'If they lived near London obviously you would have been able to meet them on a friendly basis, but asking you to come all the way to Devon makes it sound ...' He broke off again, obviously unsure how to phrase what he wanted to say.

'Sound final?' she asked coldly. 'You were afraid I would force you to an early decision?'

'No,' he protested. 'Oh, it's difficult to explain. I thought ...' He spread his wide shoulders. 'This is our marriage. Once the family were involved there would be outside influences at work.'

Her face softened. 'That's true,' she said more warmly. Then her eyes grew serious again. 'We've been seeing each other for a long time. Surely you've told your family that I'm not one of Alex's women?'

'Of course,' he said quickly. Then he hesitated. 'But you see, before I got to know you ...' The words trailed off and he gave her a quick, embarrassed look, his broad face flushed.

'What?' she asked shrewdly, staring at him.

Robin made a grimace. 'Well, when I joined the firm I heard some gossip about you and Alex ... I wrote home, just mentioning it ... and when I got to know you later of course I told my family it was all lies, but ...'

'But they didn't believe it?' Her face was hot with angry emotion.

'Mother is naturally concerned about me,' Robin said in protest. 'You go abroad with Alex such a lot ... she sees pictures of you both in the papers ... Oh, darling, you're a very beautiful girl.' His brown eyes pleaded with her. 'It isn't surprising if she can't shake off those old stories.'

Deborah finished her soup and pushed the plate away, her mind filled with conflicting emotions. 'Robin, how long did you go on believing I was ... was Alex's mistress?' Her eyes pinned him immobile, his face confused.

'I ...' He stammered, thrown. 'Only a week or two. Once I knew you I was convinced it was lies.'

Deborah knew a moment of sheer rage. The feeling seemed to fly through her body, making her tense and on the point of bursting out into violent speech. She placed her hands on the edge of the table, her fingertips white as she pressed fiercely against the wood beneath the white cloth. After a moment she said, 'I've told you frankly that I am not, and never have been, involved with Alex. Either you accept my word or you don't. Marriage can't be based on hidden suspicion.'

'I've never suspected you since ...' he began, his voice trailing away under her gaze.

'If you were quite certain about me I think your family would be, too,' she said flatly.

Robin sighed. 'Mother ...' he began, then fell silent.

'Mother,' Deborah said ironically.

'You can see her point of view,' he said quickly. 'She doesn't know you. She only knows ...'

'What you tell her,' she broke in bitterly.

'Deb, I love you,' he appealed, leaning very quickly towards her, his hand grasping at hers.

Her face was still for a second, staring at him, then the hardness drained out of her features and her blue eyes smiled at him. The warmth in his voice was convincing.

They ate their second course in more harmonious conditions than the first. Looking at Robin as he talked about one of the accounts, Deborah felt a surge of affection for him. All her life she had longed to have a home, somewhere gentle, calm and full of security. As a child at school she had seen the other girls go home for the holidays with bitter envy, hearing them talk of their families with only her own lonely days shut away out of her uncle's sight to look forward to, knowing that the only emotion her uncle felt towards her was irritation and duty. She had dreamt of belonging to someone. Meeting Robin, she had felt he offered her the sort of background she had never had—loving family surroundings, relatives, a warm concerned future. She had not missed the passion Robin never offered her. It did not enter into her view of the sort of life she desired so deeply.

Robin's strong, capable face and placid nature had attracted her whenever they met in the beginning, and when, hesitantly, he made slight overtures to her, she had responded. It had never occurred to her that gossip linked her name with that of Alex St James. She had been circumspect with him. She had put up an unbreachable wall between them, and to be blamed for doing something she had always resisted so firmly seemed bitterly unfair.

Deborah's desire for a warm family life had made her detest the idea of having an affair with anyone. She had observed Alex over the past four years, during relationships with a series of beautiful girls, and the untidy, anguished nature of such a life was alien to her. She had felt irritation, pity and scorn for his willing victims. For Alex she had felt hostility and contempt.

To her love was a word which hid a concept of life— she had no place for the wild storms of passion, the sweetness of sensuality. They were destructive, she had decided. From an early age she had avoided them.

As they drank their coffee, Robin said quietly, 'In a family as close as mine you have to expect other people to have their views about everything, Deb. You'll have to live with them, you know.'

'Do you mean that I'm on approval with your parents, Robin?' she asked sharply.

'No,' he said. 'I've told them I'm serious—they know that. But it is important that Mother likes you. I'm fond of my family. We're very close-knit and we care about each other.'

The words soothed her. It was unfair to complain when part of his real attraction for her was that close-knit family background.

She looked at him, sighing. 'I'll be on my best behaviour,' she said, half teasingly. 'I want to be friends with your mother.'

Robin relaxed. 'You'll like her. She's a very friendly person. Our house is always full of people. Mother isn't house-proud, but she does like to fill the place with friends.' He grinned at her. 'You're more domesticated than she is, Deb. I've told her what a wonderful housewife you'll make ... how tidy your flat is, despite Judith.'

She laughed. Her flatmate, Judith, was absent-minded and untidy, and their few rows came about because Judith had no idea of keeping order around her. She knew already that Robin's mother had a number of hobbies; painting flowers, playing the piano by ear, gardening. Robin had often laughed about his mother's untidiness, his tone indulgent.

'I'm sure I shall get on with your mother,' she said. 'I've heard so much about her.'

Robin looked worried. 'I haven't bored you with my family, have I? I know I tend to talk about them all the time, but a family is important, isn't it?'

'Very important,' she agreed eagerly. 'I love hearing about your family. All my life I've missed having one. I feel as if yours was mine, too.'

He smiled broadly. 'It soon will be!'

In the lift, returning to the office, Robin slid an arm around her shoulders and she turned her face towards him expectantly. Discreetly, he preferred to kiss in private, and the brief, gentle embrace bore no resemblance to the violence with which Alex had kissed her earlier. In her mind, irritably, she compared the two, telling herself she preferred Robin's controlled warmth.

Looking up at him, she asked hesitantly, 'Would it help to smooth the weekend if I told your family I was leaving my job with Alex?'

Robin looked horrified. 'Darling, you aren't, are you? You'd never earn such a good salary anywhere else! We'll need your money in the first two years after we're married, remember. The sort of house we want will be very expensive, and you know we agreed not to start a family until we could easily afford it.'

She looked at him, half despairingly. 'But if your mother thinks ...' she began faintly, but he shook his head.

'Once Mother meets you, she'll know for certain you aren't the sort of girl to fall for Alex,' he said with conviction. 'It's very convenient to have both of us working at the same place. I can run you home after work. We'll be together all day.' His brown eyes were warm as he smiled down at her, stepping out of the lift. 'It will be marvellous. We'll have a wonderful life. Our combined income will make things so much easier.'

When she entered her own office Deborah stood for a moment, frowning. Seeing a shadow on the glass between her room and that of Alex, she walked across and opened the door to inform him that she had thought better of her resignation. The thought of telling Robin her real reasons for leaving was too thorny.

Her eyes took in what she saw with a feeling of bitter

anger as Sammy Starr, her thin arms around Alex's neck, pulled her head back from the passionate kiss they were exchanging, and said, 'Hi! I've just signed my contract ... back on the old chain. Just when I was thinking of kicking the habit of adoring Alex and found a more faithful master ...'

Deborah smiled politely, her blue eyes frozen. 'Glad to be keeping you with us, Sammy,' she said, ignoring Alex's sardonic glance. 'I expected you to arrive later.'

'I talked Alex into buying me lunch,' Sammy said, pulling down her skimpy sweater. The jeans she was wearing were far too tight, but her boyishly slender body had an aggressively sensual sway as she sauntered to the door. 'See you, Alex,' she said, waving as she departed.

Alex leaned back against his desk, eyeing Deborah. 'A pity all our artists aren't as easy to handle as Sammy.'

'You manage to handle most of them,' she said pointedly.

He made a wry face. 'Sarcasm! I've just eaten a heavy lunch. Spare me the daggers, Miss Portman.' Under his thick, dark lashes his eyes observed her thoughtfully. 'Enjoy your meal with Robin?'

'Yes,' she said, nerving herself to withdraw her resignation.

'Tell him about my evil assault?' he asked, tongue in cheek.

'I didn't want to bore him with it,' she snapped.

He laughed shortly. 'Did you tell him you'd resigned?'

Her lids fell. Nervously she passed her tongue over her lips. Looking up, she saw the narrowed, shrewd eyes fixed on her.

'Out with it, Deb,' Alex said brusquely.

She felt her face flare with angry colour. He knew. She stared at him, hating him. 'I've ... I've changed my mind ...' she stammered.

'You told Robin and he was horrified,' he translated grimly.

'I earn a good salary here,' she said quickly. 'It's convenient for us both to work together ...'

'Spare me the explanations,' he shrugged. 'You withdraw your resignation.'

She burned with resentment at his dry tone. 'Yes,' she said tightly, glaring at him.

He moved closer, their eyes meeting, and she instinctively backed in apprehension. 'Aren't you afraid I'll do it again?' he asked silkily, a smile coming to his cruel mouth.

The thought had already occurred to her. She was aware of a strong sense of anxiety about the future. Distastefully, she retorted, 'If you do I'll have to tell Robin and make him see why I must leave, won't I?'

Alex laughed softly. 'Your tone of contempt amuses me, Deborah. From your tidy, neatly arranged little world you feel so secure. I wonder how hard it would be to blow a hole through the wall you've surrounded yourself with?'

She felt her throat close in panic. Turning, she said bitterly, 'I shouldn't bother. I'm proof against anything you do, Alex. You forget, I've seen you in action a hundred times before.'

He made no swift comeback to that remark, but as she left the room he said coolly, 'What time is the flight?'

'Nine o'clock,' she told him.

'I'll pick you up at seven-thirty,' he said. 'Will you get our currency?'

'I've made all the arrangements,' she said politely.

The silvery eyes mocked her. 'Of course you have. You're so efficient, Miss Portman.'

She slammed the door as she left, infuriated by his

expression and tone. Working with him in future was going to be even more impossible, she thought bitterly.

Deborah's flatmate was a twenty-four-year-old schoolteacher whom she had met two years earlier when they both attended a series of pottery classes at a London institute. Judith Brown had proved far less deft than Deborah, who had surprised herself by a natural aptitude for the subject, and through their mutual amusement at the misshapen objects Judith turned out, their friendship had grown rapidly. Deborah had at the time shared a ground-floor flat in a house in Chelsea with an Australian girl. When Penny returned to Australia after spending two years in Europe, Judith took her place, and the arrangement had worked very well. Judith taught at a school in Fulham, a bus ride from the flat, and although she had little taste for domesticity, she was a lively companion. The two girls got on well together. Deborah did most of the housework and cooking. Judith was prone to burn things through forgetting them, and her clumsiness around the flat made her accident-prone. But Deborah did not mind her friend's awkwardness because her affection for Judith made her indulgent towards her.

Judith had a number of friends, some male, who visited her often, but she had no permanent relationship in her life. Oddly, she and Robin got on very well, although he teased her about her untidiness. 'She reminds me of my mother,' he used to tell Deborah with a grin. 'She's clever, funny and absent-minded.'

Deborah walked from the bus-stop along the river, enjoying her daily view of the Thames. In all weathers it held great beauty for her. She liked to watch the changing colours of the seasons; the opalescent mists of spring, the blue of summer, the blaze of autumn and the muted grey of winter. Even in the depth of

January the river seemed to her romantic. She liked to watch the strings of tarpaulin-covered barges, the river steamers, the police boats whizzing past. Glancing back she could gaze at the layered vista of London, the towers and office blocks, the bridges and steeples. Her walks home were always pleasurable, and she knew she would regret leaving Chelsea after her marriage to Robin. His dream of a small suburban house was one she shared, but she had hidden longings about London which she slightly resented. Although the city was beautiful it was lonely, as she had found in earlier years, and she could not quite understand why, despite this, she felt so drawn towards it.

She had packed and was cooking supper when Judith arrived, hot and flushed from her journey, her wiry ginger hair tumbling over her narrow shoulders as she looked into the tiny kitchen.

They shared a sitting-room from which two tiny bedrooms led, besides a kitchen and a bathroom so small they had to squeeze into it.

'What's for supper? I'm starving,' Judith said, sniffing.

'Vegetable soup and a cheese soufflé,' Deborah told her. 'It uses up the last of our cheese.'

'Smells great,' grinned Judith. 'Have I got time to wash and change?'

'Ten minutes,' Deborah told her, and Judith vanished.

When she returned, her hair tied with a green velvet ribbon, her body sheathed in a black catsuit, she sat down on a kitchen chair with a groan. 'My feet ache. Going out with Robin tonight?'

'No,' said Deborah. 'Lay the table for me, Judith.'

Judith made a face. 'If I can move,' she said, pathetically. 'There must be easier jobs than teaching. Like sweeping the streets or scrubbing floors.'

'Stop moaning and lay the table,' said Deborah, unimpressed. She pushed the cutlery into Judith's hand and the other girl obediently went into their sitting-room. From there, she called, 'Alex come back today, did he?'

Deborah paused, staring into the bubbling soup, her face taut, a hot flush pouring up her cheeks. The sound of his name recalled the way Alex had kissed her with vivid detail, and anger and shame made her bite her lip.

A sound brought her head round. Judith was staring at her from the archway of the sitting-room, her hazel eyes narrowed.

'What happened?' the other girl asked bluntly.

Deborah turned and turned off the light under the soup. 'What do you mean?' she fenced, busily engaged in pouring the soup into a tureen.

'Deb, I saw your expression,' Judith said, her voice flat. 'Only Alex St James brings that look into your eyes.'

'What look?' Deborah stared at her, taken aback.

Judith shrugged, half embarrassed. 'I don't know how to describe it . . . helpless, sort of . . . vulnerable.'

'Oh, nonsense,' Deborah dismissed abruptly, moving into the sitting-room.

They sat opposite each other at the small table in the bay of their sitting-room window. Deborah helped Judith to soup and then placed some in her own bowl.

Judith broke off a small piece of crispbread and fiddled with it, her soup untouched. 'I gather Alex did get back from Stockholm, though?' she enquired.

'Yes,' said Deborah, her gaze on her spoon. 'But we're going to France tomorrow, so you'll have to do the shopping. I'll make up a list of what we need.'

'France!' Judith's gaze was curious. 'I thought you were going to Devon this weekend to meet Robin's family? What about the engagement announcement?'

Deborah said coolly, 'It all goes ahead as planned. I'll be back on Friday evening.'

'What did Robin say when you told him?' asked Judith probingly.

Deborah sighed. 'He understood,' she lied.

Judith made a peculiar sound, something between a snort and a grunt.

'What's that supposed to mean?' Deborah demanded.

'Nothing,' said Judith. 'It isn't my business.'

'No,' Deborah said, 'it isn't.'

Judith began to drink her soup. The course was finished in silence. As Judith began to clear the bowls, Deborah said with a sigh, 'I'm sorry, Judy ... I snapped.'

Judith looked down and her face split into a warm smile. 'Oh, I forgive you. You know your own business best. I get worried about you sometimes. You're like a single-minded child walking across a busy street. You look neither to left nor right, you just march straight into disaster.'

Deborah laughed with amusement. 'Judy, that describes you rather than me ... I thought I was the levelheaded one, the one who knew what she wanted out of life, while you just rush from one crisis to the other without thinking.'

Judy's face was sober. 'Your plans are too cut and dried, Deb. They leave no room for life at all. You won't allow anything to interfere with your carefully worked out scheme of living, and that's dangerous. I'm afraid that one day a volcano will explode right under your feet and blow you sky-high.'

Deborah stared at her in astonishment. 'What on earth are you talking about?'

'Alex St James,' said Judith, holding her eyes. 'You know I'm talking about him.'

Scarlet invaded Deborah's face. Her eyes widened,

then her lids dropped, hiding her expression. She moved quickly into the kitchen and without thinking picked up oven gloves and got the soufflé out of the oven. It was perfectly risen, a smooth golden colour. She carried it into the sitting-room and placed it on a mat in the centre of the table. Judith was laying plates, her untidy bush of hair falling over one shoulder.

Deborah served the soufflé and they each took their seats again. A bowl of fresh, crisp salad occupied the centre of the table. Deborah helped herself to some, her eyes fixed on what she was doing.

'No comment, then?' Judith asked at last.

'Your imagination runs riot,' Deborah said without looking at her.

'Deb, because Robin has never noticed your sensitivity to Alex St James it doesn't mean you've learnt to hide it from everyone,' Judith told her frankly. 'I knew the first time I saw you together. You admitted years ago that he fancied you.'

'I didn't say that!' Deborah denied.

'You said he wanted to date you,' Judith said flatly. 'Don't forget, I've seen him look at you. He makes no secret of the way he feels.'

'Oh, for heaven's sake!' Deborah said furiously. 'Alex flirts with every woman he meets. I know, I've seen him in action every day. How many beautiful women do you think he's been to bed with? I doubt if even Alex can remember. Do you think I'm going to be a forgotten name in his telephone book, one of the never-ending list who couldn't resist him?' Her voice rose, bitterness threaded through it.

Judith looked at her with a strange expression. 'So you made up your mind to be the one girl he can't forget, the one who got away?' she asked shrewdly.

For a moment Deborah looked stunned. Then a weary smile came into the blue eyes. 'Something like that,' she admitted huskily.

Judith made a face. 'I hope you get away with it,' she said, beginning to eat her soufflé. She sighed. 'This is a dream. When I tried to make a soufflé it just lay there in the oven glowering at me!'

'What do you mean,' Deborah pursued, 'you hope I get away with it?'

Judith swallowed her mouthful. 'You're walking a tightrope, Deb,' she said gently. 'If Robin ever finds out how you really feel about Alex he'll feel cheated, and if Alex ever finds out, God help you!'

'I love Robin,' Deborah protested, staring at her. 'I mean, I've never cheated him. I don't love Alex ... I don't, Judith.'

'Maybe you don't,' Judith conceded. 'But I know you, Deb. You're very attracted to him—far more than you are to Robin. When you're with Alex you're on edge the whole time, as tense as a bowstring. If he touches you, you jump. I'd have to be deaf, dumb and blind not to see how aware you are of him. Yet Robin can spend a whole evening alone with you in the flat and you look as calm as a nun after evensong ... if you really loved Robin you would have been tempted to go to bed with him by now, but you two sit and watch television as if you've been married for years. Good lord, you're more like brother and sister than lovers!'

The accusation left Deborah speechless. She pushed away her plate, her meal uneaten. After a pause, she said lamely, 'No one can see inside a relationship. You don't know anything about how Robin and I feel.'

'That may be true,' Judith said in a gentle voice. 'I'm fond of you, Deb. I hate to think you may get hurt. But marrying someone you don't love deeply can be a painful mistake ... for both of you. You must be sure about it before you decide. For Robin's sake, if not for your own.'

Deborah nervously stood up. 'You can hardly say we've rushed into anything. Robin and I know each other better than most married couples.'

'Ask yourself one question—does Robin's lovemaking excite you?' Judith persisted.

Deborah flushed. 'That's a very personal question. You may be looking for passion in your marriage, but passion fades. Real affection doesn't. I want a marriage based on affection, not on passion.'

Judith made a shrugging acceptance. 'But does Robin?' she said on a sigh.

Deborah smiled. 'Like myself, he wants his feet on the ground, not his head in the clouds.'

Judith nodded, staring at the bowl of salad. 'Maybe you're right. Maybe you and Robin are suited. I hope so.'

As Deborah made coffee she was deep in thought. It was the second time today that someone had questioned her engagement to Robin, and although she discounted everything Alex had said, automatically, knowing that his barbed remarks were based on his hurt vanity because he could not believe anyone could prefer Robin to himself, Judith's words were more disturbing. During the two years they had shared a flat, she had come to trust and like her flatmate more than any other girl she had ever known. Judith was untidy, clumsy, impulsive, but she had quick wit, intelligence and warmth, and Deborah dared not ignore her remarks.

Was there some truth in what Judith had said? She admitted to herself that she had always been aware of her own reluctant attraction to Alex. Alex had made no secret of his appreciation of her, either, his silvery eyes bluntly approving her looks. She had always felt as if the ground between them was mined. An unwary step might precipitate an explosion. But physical awareness was no basis for a serious relationship. She refused to enter into the sort of brief liaison Alex always had with women. The idea disgusted her. It had seemed only common sense to avoid him altogether.

She still felt she was right, but Judith's reference to cheating Robin worried her. If she admitted to Robin that she ... her face flamed as she baulked at putting into words how she felt about Alex. If Robin ever suspected the truth, wouldn't he think she could not love him? She put her hands to her hot face. Could she love Robin while feeling as she did about Alex? The two men were as different as chalk to cheese. She admired everything about Robin, she told herself. She trusted him, she enjoyed his company, she liked him ... Despairingly, she said, in a whisper, 'I love him.' Horribly afraid that her words bore no ring of confidence. Surely it was true that love was based on knowledge, respect, admiration, rather than on violent physical awareness?

Taking the coffee in to Judith, she sank down and stared at her, her blue eyes almost desperate. 'I don't even like Alex,' she told her suddenly.

Judith made no reply, but compassion filled her face as she looked back at her.

CHAPTER THREE

AFTER London's intermittent sunshine and showers Nice looked as unreal and beautiful as a coloured postcard; the streets lined with palm trees whose leaves were green and lustrous, the hotels dazzlingly white and glinting in the sun, the layered rows of houses softly washed in pastel colours, over all of the town the brilliant azure sky making it look more like a film set than anything Deborah could remember. They drove from the airport in a hired car which she had booked from London. Alex knew the route well from previous visits, his long hands capable on the wheel, his hard profile abstracted in thought.

'Your mother lives near here, doesn't she?' asked Deborah, oddly irritated by his apparent unawareness of her presence beside him in the car.

He turned his head, the dark hair brushing against the collar of the dark brown shirt he wore.

'Yes,' he agreed vaguely. The silvery eyes skimmed over her, observing the cool turquoise linen dress she wore. A faint flush rose in her face, and his mouth curved suddenly in mockery.

'My mother lives an hour's drive from here,' he said. 'She has an idyllic cottage beside the river, miles from any other habitation.' His voice held a strange note of irony, which she noted.

'Doesn't she get lonely?'

'She's a painter,' he said, as if that explained everything.

'What sort of painter?'

He shrugged, turning back to his interest in the

traffic around them. 'Largely still life. She paints flowers a good deal. She does portraits occasionally, but she has no real talent for them. Her still lifes sell well though.'

Deborah was curious. 'Enough to live on?'

He laughed. 'I doubt it. She isn't that good. She takes them to an art dealer in Nice who sells them to rich tourists. They make Mother a pleasant addition to her income, that's all.'

Deborah wondered if he supported his mother financially, and imagined he must be doing so. Certainly he earned enough. The firm was largely in his possession, and although he lived well he must be very well off, she supposed. It had never occurred to her to be interested in his background. That his family had owned the firm had given him the sort of secure, moneyed background which explained his air of arrogant self-assurance.

'Do you see much of your mother?' she asked, as he spun the car into the curved drive leading to their hotel.

'My mother isn't a gregarious soul,' he said tersely.

She wondered what that meant, unclipping her safety belt and opening the car door. Alex came round and assisted her to alight, his hand beneath her elbow. A group of strolling holidaymakers passed them, laughing, their air of leisure underlining their reason for being here. Deborah looked after them enviously. The two women wore brief sun-dresses and large straw hats, their bodies smoothly tanned.

Alex glanced after them, then looked down at her wryly. 'Wish you were here on holiday?' he asked.

'The weather is wonderful,' she sighed. 'Nice must be marvellous for a honeymoon.'

Alex's hand tightened around her elbow and she

made a silent face of protest, her lips parting in a wince.

He turned to greet the hotel doorman, in his smart uniform, who came hurrying to meet them.

Their rooms were side by side on the first floor, facing the sea, each with french windows leading out on to a shared balcony. A page boy escorted them, carrying their luggage. While he was showing Alex his room she opened the french windows in her own and went out on to the balcony to stare down the white promenade, through the smooth leaves of palm trees, to where the blue water curled on to the beach.

Half-naked bodies lay under beach umbrellas in the cool shade which protected them from the direct rays of the sun. A few people were swimming. One or two were sailing in small dinghies, the white of the sails flapping in a faint breeze. She could just hear the jingle of the mast wires as they turned.

A step brought her attention back to her more immediate surroundings. She turned and met Alex's silvery eyes. She was surprised to see that he had already changed into pale lightweight slacks and a brief black T-shirt, the silver medallion Sammy had given him still dangling around his brown throat.

'You've changed,' she said unnecessarily.

His brows lifted sardonically. 'So I have,' he mocked. His eyes slid down over her. 'You'd better do the same. You look too neat and businesslike in that dress. Surely you brought something more casual?'

Deborah flushed. 'Only jeans and a top,' she admitted. 'I hadn't expected it to be so warm.'

'Put them on,' he commanded.

Irritated by his tone, she turned away, halting as he asked softly, 'Do you realise we're sharing a bathroom? You're slipping, Miss Portman. You usually manage to get us rooms on different floors, let alone side by side.'

'The booking was so late,' she said crossly. 'I had to take what they offered me.'

'Irritating for you,' he said in that tone which held a taunting amusement. Before she had a chance to retort, he added, 'I've just rung Ricky Winter and he's invited us to his villa for dinner. We'll have the day free until seven, so we might as well lunch downstairs and then take a look around Nice.'

She hesitated, alarmed at the prospect of spending so long alone with Alex in this warm, slumbrous atmosphere.

He was watching her, his silvery eyes half hidden by his lids. 'Are you afraid to be alone with me, Miss Portman?' he asked in that insidiously soft voice.

She clenched her hands at her side, longing to slap his face. 'Don't be ridiculous,' she said stiffly.

'Then go and get changed,' he said lightly.

She went back into her room, pausing to look at the open french windows with consideration, yet not daring, while Alex actually stood out there on the balcony to close and bolt them.

Finding her case, she laid it on the bed and began to unpack her clothes. She had brought the bare minimum with her, and frowned over them reluctantly, before hanging up the one evening dress she had brought, then getting out her jeans and top. When she had finished transferring the other items to drawers, she went into the bathroom.

It had two doors, she found. The one leading into Alex's room she bolted, then bolted her own, before beginning to wash and change her clothes.

Refreshed, slender in her casual clothes, she eyed herself in the bathroom mirror, hesitating over the skimpy and revealing white cotton top. What on earth had possessed her to pack it? she asked herself in despair.

It had been a last-minute decision which she now regretted.

After a moment she unbolted the doors and slowly went back to the balcony. Alex sat there on a white-painted wicker chair, reading a newspaper which, she saw with some surprise, was in French.

He looked up, after a few seconds, and they stared at each other with the wary appraisal of animals. His eyes moved over her with leisurely curiosity. The silvery depths held no expression, but she shifted uneasily under his gaze.

'You look like a different girl,' he said slowly. His tone held a faint surprise. His eyes moved back to her white top. Sleeveless, cut in a plunging scoop which revealed the pale swell of her breasts, it was almost transparent in this strong sunshine, moulding her body like a second skin, but leaving a narrow gap between where it ended and where her jeans began, so that her smooth midriff could be glimpsed whenever she moved. Under his intent gaze she felt half naked and moved restlessly. 'Shall we go down to lunch?'

He rose, glancing at his wristwatch. 'A little early, but why not? We'll have more time on the beach.'

'The beach?' Her question was abrupt.

'You seemed envious of those holidaymakers,' he drawled. 'A few hours on the beach might be fun.'

They went along the thickly carpeted corridor in silence. Alex jabbed the lift button with his forefinger, and a few seconds later the lift arrived. They stepped inside. The doors closed silently, but when the lift started it gave a violent jerk, throwing Deborah sideways. Alex stopped her from falling by receiving her against his chest. Off balance, she lay against him, automatically reaching towards his shoulders to support herself. Through the fine cotton of her top she felt the strong muscles beneath his shirt, the animal warmth of his skin against her, and her heart began to race violently. His hands came around her, enclosing her, his palms laid flat against her back, one long thumb beginning to move in sensual massage along the exposed skin above her top. Deborah was unable to pull herself away. The moment elongated, leaving her curiously weak, intensely conscious of the firm muscles of his thighs against her legs.

A sick sensation came up into her throat. She pulled herself together and moved away from him, her eyes lowered in self-disgust, shuddering as she realised how she had felt during their contact.

In the past Alex had been apt to make one of his barbed comments on such occasions. She was puzzled and surprised when he made no remark on what happened, half turned away from her as the lift came to a halt.

Was he unaware of how she had felt? she wondered, following him across the wide, busy foyer to the dining-room. Spacious, carpeted, half empty at this early hour, the room looked out on to the sea front, tubs of blazing red geraniums lining the steps beyond the window. A billiard-table-smooth green lawn stretched down to a low wall. Beyond Deborah could see people walking in a lazy fashion along the pavement.

They sat down facing each other at a table near the window, and she pretended to be absorbed in the view, unwiling to risk meeting Alex's eyes.

When the menu was handed to her she was able to hide behind that, nervousness prickling in her throat.

They ate in comparative silence, avoiding looking at each other. Alex had ordered an excellent wine with the meal, and despite her protests, he insisted on topping up her glass from time to time. She drank very little, and the wine began to affect her, making her relax as the meal progressed, giving her false courage, so that she felt able to meet his unreadable eyes.

Deciding that his mother made a safe topic of conversation, she asked brightly, 'Will you ring your mother while you're here? She could come into Nice for lunch tomorrow.'

He looked up from his lobster salad, his eyes narrowing. 'I'll certainly ring her,' he said. 'Whether she'll come into Nice is another matter. Mother hates leaving her cottage.'

'Even to see you?' she asked teasingly.

'Even to see me,' he assented drily.

She looked at him curiously. 'Don't you get on with your mother?' She bit her lip. 'I'm sorry, I shouldn't have asked.'

He shrugged. 'Why not? Yes, I get on with her well enough. We have our own lives, though, and we make it a rule never to interfere with each other.'

She frowned. It was so unlike the sort of family life she needed and admired. 'But she's your mother...' Her tone revealed her disbelief and disapproval.

He smiled grimly. 'That doesn't make it necessary for us to live in each other's pockets.'

'You must hurt her feelings by being so indifferent,' she said, her blue eyes critical.

'Who said I was indifferent?' he asked. 'If I thought for a moment she needed me I'd drop everything and go to her at once. Mother knows that. And I know she would come if I wanted her.' His gaze measured her comprehension coolly. 'All families aren't identical, you know.'

'Robin's family are very close-knit,' she said enthusiastically.

'What about yours?' he asked her, his mouth dented.

Her eyes saddened. 'I have no one,' she said, her voice reflecting her regret.

Alex frowned. 'No relatives at all?' The silvery eyes

narrowed on her face in hard observation.

She shook her head. 'Neither of my parents had anyone. Except an uncle. He brought me up when they died. He was more interested in his stamp collection than in human beings.'

'How old were you when your parents died?' he asked, accepting the smooth orange cream the waiter brought him with a nod.

'A baby,' she said shortly, beginning to eat her own sweet, a fluffy concoction of soft strawberries and ice-cream embedded in whipped cream. It was too sweet for her taste, and after a while she pushed it away.

'So you were brought up by a rather remote uncle?' he persisted, finishing his own course and leaning back.

The waiter appeared, bowing, and they ordered coffee. Alex asked her permission to smoke a thin cigar, and lit it, his strong-fingered hands deft.

'Do you really think jeans are suitable for the beach?' Deborah asked, aware, as she watched his hands, that she was alarmed at the idea of spending time with him in such relaxing surroundings.

He looked at her over his cigar, pale blue smoke wreathing around his dark head. A smile smouldered in the depths of the silvery eyes. 'We'll see about that later,' he said ambiguously.

As they crossed the foyer after lunch he took her elbow and guided her towards the hotel shop which held pride of place at the back of the carpeted floor. Puzzled, she allowed him to guide her through the door. Was he buying a gift for his mother? she wondered, as the svelte young assistant sauntered towards them.

'A bikini for the young lady,' Alex murmured.

'No!' Deborah exclaimed, flushing. 'I don't need ...'

He smiled at the assistant. 'That one will do, if you

have her size,' he said, jerking his head towards one on display.

Deborah's eyes widened in horror as she looked at it. She had never worn anything so revealing in her life. 'No,' she said again, in deeper rejection. But the girl was smiling, her eyes amused, and she moved away to return in an instant with a small box. Gesturing to a tiny fitting-room, she invited Deborah to try the bikini on in privacy.

Alex said, taking her arm and turning her so that the assistant should not hear, 'Do you want me to put it on you myself?'

She felt her cheeks burn. 'I can't wear that thing,' she protested.

'Stop being tiresome,' he said in a bored tone. He pushed her towards the fitting-room, thrusting the box into her hands.

She looked at herself in the long mirror a few moments later with flushed incredulity. Against her white skin the black brevity of the silky material showed like shadows. Fine silken cords linked the two tiny cups of the top, revealing the soft, high swell of her breasts. The briefs were tied at the hip in the same manner and left nothing whatever to the imagination. She felt naked.

A voice behind the drawn curtain asked curtly, 'Have you tried it on yet?'

'Yes,' she said with angry embarrassment. 'It ... it's absurd ... I couldn't wear it!'

'Show me,' he said.

'No!' she cried at once, her voice throbbing with panic.

Alex drew the curtain with a rattle of brass rings, and she backed, her face scarlet.

He looked at her slowly from head to foot. 'My God,' he said huskily. 'You're superb!'

The words were like a caress. She quivered at them, wanting to hide from the possessive touch of his eyes.

'Don't be afraid of your own body, Deb,' he said gently. 'Hasn't anyone ever told you that you're beautiful?'

She nervously ran her tongue over her lips and he watched her, fastening his gaze on the tiny movement in a way which made her more nervous than ever.

Thrusting another box at her, he said, 'Try this on, too.'

Before she could protest he had drawn the curtain and gone again. Perhaps, she thought hopefully, it was a less revealing swimsuit. She opened it and found a beach-coat which matched the bikini, made in the same colour and material. It might at least, she thought, conceal the brevity of what she wore, so she shook it out and slid into it.

It had a tie-belt and lapels which only just covered the swell of her breasts, and it ended mid-thigh, but it made her feel less naked. Through the curtain Alex said mockingly, 'Feel safer, Deborah?'

She made no answer. She untied the belt and carefully packed the garment away, then hurriedly got dressed again. When she drew the curtain Alex was talking to the assistant some feet away, his charming smile bent on her appreciative face.

He turned as Deborah walked towards them. She held out the two boxes, her speech prepared, ready to refuse them.

'I've paid for them,' he said coolly. 'I got some beach sandals, too.' He took the boxes from her, pushed them under his arm, smiling at the assistant, saying a few words in rapid French to her, before he pushed Deborah out of the shop.

In the foyer she dragged her feet, angrily telling him,

'How dare you buy that thing for me? I didn't want it. I shall take it back!'

'You'll need it tomorrow,' he retorted calmly. 'It's probable that we'll have to go out to Ricky's villa in the morning for further discussions, and judging by the clothes you normally wear your idea of swimsuits will do nothing for his temperature.'

He pulled her, reluctantly, into the lift and the doors closed. Deborah flushed, seeing curious eyes on them as they vanished, several people in the foyer having seen their progress, in open conflict, across the floor.

Turning on Alex, she wrenched her arm from his grasp. 'Just for the record, I'm not here as a toy for Ricky Winter. I came to help you persuade him to sign with us, not to seduce him!'

He grinned. 'What gives you the idea I want you to seduce him? Just look alluring and smile at him ... that's all you have to do. It will set a co-operative atmosphere. Ricky's susceptible to lovely women.'

'You have no moral inhibitions, do you?' she asked bitterly. 'Why don't you offer him an honest deal?'

'I shall do,' he shrugged. 'But I know human beings. Women buy cosmetics because they're taken by the pretty wrappings.' The long, considering glance swept over her. 'And your wrappings are very pretty.'

She tingled with irritation. 'If you insist on buying those things I shall have to pay for them. I'm not accepting presents from you.'

'I'll stop them from your next cheque,' he said, unmoved by the insult in her voice. 'I'll get my swimming trunks and beach towel, then we'll go down to the beach. The hotel has a private section of sand and its own changing cabins.'

Half an hour later Deborah emerged from the tiny cabin to find Alex standing at the edge of the water in black trunks, staring out across the blue sea. Unlike herself, he was bronzed by the sun, the hard lean body fit and athletic, his broad shoulders and smooth-skinned back tapering to slim hips and long, muscled thighs. Reluctantly she walked towards him, conscious of the glances she was getting from some of the young men playing beach-ball over a fixed net a few yards away. One of them gave a low whistle, calling something to her in French.

Alex turned. He watched her walk forward, acutely embarrassed by the brevity of the black bikini, but angrily defiant both of herself and the observer. Her fine blonde hair floated around her shoulders in a silken curtain which brushed her bare skin as she moved.

'You look five years younger,' he murmured as she joined him. Dry-mouthed, she glanced at the bare brown chest, roughened by fine dark hair, against which the silver medallion swung as he breathed. 'I think I'll swim right away,' she said, diving into the water.

He followed her, his dark head appearing in the waves in front of her, rising and sinking above the sea, his arms moving rhythmically over his head.

He was already on the raft when she arrived. Fixed some way from the beach, it was further than she had realised, and Alex had to lean down, his muscular hand gripping her wrist, to haul her aboard. Water streamed from her hair as she sat down beside him, the long wet strands clinging to her face. She breathed faster than usual, tired by the swim. The sparkle of the sun on the water dazzled her eyes for a moment. She gazed back at the beach, watching the glitter of hotel windows, the shimmering vista of palm trees, white buildings, small figures on the sands.

Alex was sitting there casually, his long legs dangling in the water. He suddenly pushed back her damp, darkened hair with a casual hand, and the touch woke a sweetness in her which made her turn on him, her voice cutting. 'Don't touch me!' The response was instinctive, angry, self-protective.

His smile vanished. There were sparks in the grey eyes. 'You've been saying that for too long. I'm sick of hearing it!' His hands grabbed her, digging into the sunwarmed, wet flesh until she gasped.

'Alex, don't!' she said in real alarm, but he pushed her backwards despite her attempt to resist, until her back met the raft, his body pressing her down on to the hard planks, his hands holding her head in a vice as she fought him, twisting sideways to escape.

Their eyes stared, locked in a silent duel, then his lowered to her parted lips and she was as conscious of that look as if he kissed her. She couldn't get away, the lean thigh muscles anchored her firmly beneath him, the broad shoulders pinned her down so that she couldn't move. Alex's fingers moved, slowly sifting through the damp fronds of her long hair. She could feel the rapid pace of her heart against her breast, and in the sunny silence trapping them together she could hear the thud of his heart above her.

Admitting defeat, she lay still, watching him. The violence seemed to have gone out of him. His hands shifted along her cheek, the fingers gentle, sensitively caressing her skin until one drew softly along the quivering line of her mouth, outlining it as if he were curious about the feel and shape of it. Deborah's hands were tensed against the wide brown shoulders, but she made no further move to escape. The warmth of his body percolated to her own, their wet skin touching, the strong thighs and calves pressed against her salt-bloomed legs.

She struggled to conjure up Robin's image, but her mind could not hold the picture. It slid away into the deep blue of the sky which arched over them. She was only aware of the rocking of the raft beneath her back, the slow erotic movements of Alex's hand across her face.

'Robin ...' she said, forcing the name to her lips in an effort to bring herself back from the brink of utter subjection.

'Damn Robin,' snapped Alex, in sudden harshness.

'I'm going to marry him,' she whispered desperately.

'Are you?' he asked lazily, and his damnable seductive fingers slid gently over her throat, coaxing her very skin to respond to them, until he bent his head without any appearance of haste, making her wait, her heart thudding, and his lips silkily tingled over the sensitised skin he had been caressing, making her eyes close in abrupt weakness.

Horrified by her shameful subjection, she opened her eyes again quickly. 'I don't want you to ...' she lied fiercely.

'No?' There was laughter in his voice. He ran his hand over her shoulders, searching out the frail hollows between her fine bones.

She descended from wrath to pleading, her voice trembling. 'Alex, stop, please ...' She was more afraid of herself than of him at that moment, humiliatingly aware that she was aching to touch him as he was touching her, her palms sweating against his shoulders, shifting restlessly, possessed by a desire to move over him in a caress. Casual lovemaking of the kind Alex indulged in had always disgusted her. How, she asked herself bitterly, could she now be torn between a physical need which was becoming urgent, and her moral principles?

Ignoring her, the deft fingers travelled searchingly over her breasts, then with an incredulous leap of realisation she felt him begin to loosen the laces be-

DUEL OF DESIRE

tween the small black cups. 'No!' Her back arched in protest. Her hands dug into his chest, the nails tearing at him. He took her hands by the slender wrists and without an effort pulled them away, folding them around his neck so that her arms encircled his head. Her angry eyes stared into his, seeing the cool determined mockery in the silvery eyes. She drew her arms down, but he had already freed her breasts and her own reaction defeated her.

Her eyes closed in the shock of a pleasure so intense it made her dizzy. The sun burnt against her closed lids, making whirling golden patterns, great sunbursts, against her retina. The strong, sensitive fingers had taken possession. She felt her breasts swell passionately into the soft cup of his hand and experienced her first moment of intense sexual excitement. It seemed to run over her skin like fire, making her molten with desire. Her trembling hands clenched in on themselves as she tried to struggle out of his hypnotic hold over her.

'You're beautiful,' he whispered. 'How can you be ashamed of so desirable a body?'

She forced her eyes to open, blinking under the sun, his head a dark Byzantine mask poised above her, the features powerful with triumph and arrogance.

'I don't want you to touch me,' she said, carrying no conviction. 'I love Robin.'

'You've never loved him,' he said, his mouth hardening.

'I don't love you,' she said, answering his expression rather than his words.

'You want me,' he said softly, 'as much as I want you. We've both known it for years.'

Shock held her silent, then she swallowed. 'Your vanity is pathetic,' she said at last, trying to smile scornfully.

'Don't lie to me Deb,' he said, untouched by her

scorn. 'Admit I could have you if I paid your price.'

'Price?' She uttered the word in flushed anger. 'What the hell do you mean?'

'Marriage,' he said coolly. 'You have quaint old-fashioned notions about getting married, don't you, Deb?'

'This is a pointless discussion,' she said irritably. 'Let go of me, Alex. You're annoying me!'

'Is that what I'm doing?' he asked mockingly. 'The rate your heart has been beating at I'd have described it quite another way.' His hands trapped her face and her traitorous heart beat violently. 'Oh, God, I want you.' he said suddenly, his voice thickening.

His words and husky voice were like a signal to her repressed emotions. As his mouth sought hers she met his lips with famished hunger, her hands reaching for his body in frantic movements of restless passion, experimentally finding where the strong neck met the unward lift of his head, the tense muscles of shoulder and arm, the long powerful back which curved down to his hips, his skin wet with salt under her fingertips. Everything else fled from her mind. Their lips fused endlessly, her softness yielding to the fierce demand of the cruel mouth, beyond protest, drugged by unknown sensual reactions, abject, mindless, only conscious of the erotic pressures of hands, lips, body. Their caresses grew fevered, an exchanged passion which underlined that Alex had spoken the truth when he had said he could have her if he wanted her.

A power boat speeding towards them from the misty reaches of the sea awoke her from the trance in which his lovemaking had held her. Her eyes flew open and she gave a low shivering cry. Alex lifted his head, silently taking in her horrified, shamed expression, then a wry smile flickered over his face.

Without a word he flung himself over on to his back,

breathing hard, staring up at the halcyon blue of the sky.

Sick, humiliated, burning with self-contempt, Deborah sat up and dived into the sea. Without thinking she swam back towards the beach. The last few moments had been a revelation to her. She had always been secretly aware that she was attracted to Alex. Now she had to face the fact that he had a power over her senses which made her despise herself.

As she walked back towards the changing hut she saw a familiar, graceful figure dismounting from a low-slung open-topped sports car, leaping over the door, disdaining to open it, the slim body tightly encased in very brief white shorts belted below the waist and a thin yellow top. Judging from the exclamations and stares he was receiving, half the beach population had recognised him too, but, flinging back his sun-whitened hair, he ignored the interest he was causing and sauntered along the promenade towards their hotel. Ricky Winter, Deborah thought. Was he calling on them? Hesitantly, she glanced back over the sea. Alex's figure could still be seen lying on the raft, his dark trunks and brown body distantly visible.

'Mr Winter!' Her voice came apologetically, her face flushed as she saw the looks she got from bystanders. She ran after him, barefoot, her wet hair flying back from her shoulders.

He glanced, a bored, irritated expression making his face look older than his years, then a new gleam came into the green eyes. He gave her a lazy smile. 'I'm not giving autographs today.' The thin, attractive face reflected amused interest. 'Sorry, darling.' He had a faint London accent overlaid by years of travelling the world. Although he was in his early twenties he had been a star for most of his adolescence and had acquired an international gloss.

'I'm Alex St James's assistant,' she said breathlessly. 'I thought you might be going to our hotel.'

He looked surprised, then smiled. 'I wasn't, actually,' he told her. 'I came into Nice to buy shoes. But they can wait.' His eyes were flatteringly approving of the black bikini. 'What's your name, Alex St James's assistant?'

'Deborah Portman,' she said, flushing slightly. 'Mr St James is out on that raft...' pointing behind him.

'Him I can wait to see,' he dismissed. 'How about coming for a drink, Deborah?' He looked down at her body. 'You'll have to change, unfortunately. You should always wear bikinis. With a body like yours clothes are wasted.'

She was aware of heat under her facial skin. 'Thank you, but I'm here to work,' she said, trying not to sound stiff, remembering that Alex had brought her here to be friendly towards this conceited young man.

Ricky wrinkled his nose in disarming and amused recognition of her reaction. 'Is that what you call work?' He wound her wet hair around a finger. 'I've heard Alex has a way with women. I approve of his taste.'

Although he was insolent and self-assured, his youth made him far less alarming than Alex, and she felt faintly touched by the swagger with which he carried off his blatant flattery. Despite his undoubted experience of life, he was still much younger than she was both in age and looks. He was slightly built, a thin boy, brash, vain but charming.

'Will you be coming to dinner tonight?' he asked.

'Yes,' she said, wondering how to disentangle her hair from his wandering fingers without rudeness.

'We'll have to get to know each other better,' he said, smiling at her. 'Is your natural colour blonde or do you have it dyed, like me? My hair was mousy brown when I was a kid.'

'My hair is natural,' she said shyly.

'The rest of you's natural, too,' he said directly, admiring her figure in a way which made her acutely self-conscious.

'Hallo, Ricky,' said a cool voice at her back.

Deborah felt herself tense. Ricky let go of her hair and gave Alex a nod. 'I was just chatting up your assistant,' he said. 'Smooth flight to Nice, was it? I bet the weather's horrible in London.' He looked ostentatiously at his wristwatch. 'God, I'm late. Sorry, I've got to rush—I've got an appointment. See you tonight, Alex.' He winked at Deborah as he passed her. 'And I'm looking forward to seeing you again, sunshine.'

When he had gone she slowly looked at Alex. His expression was impossible to read. Coolly, he said, 'Shall we change and do some sightseeing?'

'I'm tired,' she said flatly. 'I think I'll rest for a few hours at the hotel. We left London at nine and already it seems we've been here for days.'

He shrugged. 'If you insist.'

When she had changed she returned to the hotel alone, leaving Alex to amuse himself, and relaxed for some time on her bed, the curtains drawn but the french windows open to admit a cooling breeze from the sea. She was aching with angry self-condemnation. How could she have permitted herself to respond to Alex like that? She despised herself for her collapse before his practised techniques. He knew exactly how to arouse women. The sensuality of his lovemaking had not been learnt overnight. She had always been so determined not to let herself weaken towards him. How could she have done it?

Was it impossible to control the treacherous impulses of the body with the calm reason of the mind?

She thought about her relationship with Robin, her eyes troubled. When they were together it seemed exactly what she wanted—the quiet affection of partnership, the undemanding warmth which could deepen in time to strong love. She liked Robin. She had always believed such affection was more powerful and sane than her occasional anguished awareness of Alex.

Her eyes stared at the curtains blowing in the sea breeze. Frowning, she deliberately placed Robin out there on the raft with her, imagined him kissing her ... and knew it was absurd. Robin had never showed urgency, desire or violence when he made love to her. His kisses were ... she broke off, biting her lip. Like those of a brother? The phrase had come unbidden and she groaned, turning over and burying her face in the pillow.

Gradually she fell into a light doze, from which she awoke when a hand touched her shoulder.

She turned quickly, still half asleep, her lids flickering up the strong column of his lean body.

'Alex?'

'Time to get ready,' he said, his hands in his pockets.

She lay, as tense as a trapped animal, her eyes wide now. 'I'll get dressed then,' she said, waiting for him to leave.

She felt he was on the point of saying something, but at last with a derisive smile he left, and she moved off the bed reluctantly to get ready.

CHAPTER FOUR

The evening dress Deborah had brought with her was new, a recent purchase, which Judith had talked her into buying during one of their joint shopping expeditions. She had never worn it before, and now, staring at herself with dismay, she wished vainly she had brought one of the other two she owned. She often had to wear attractive evening dresses because her job entailed a good deal of entertaining, and in the past she had always bought pretty, but demure, gowns. She had been doubtful about this one when Judith persuaded her to buy it, but it looked even more revealing as she eyed her reflection.

The material was a delicate silk, turquoise, a colour deeper than the blue of her eyes but accenting them. Fragile strips of silk crossed her bare shoulders, suspending the tight bodice. There was practically no back to the dress. It clung to her body like a smooth glove, emphasising every curve, forcing her to walk slowly, her hips swaying with the constriction placed upon her movements by the material.

She had dressed her hair to fall in a smooth golden skein from the top of her head, an oval diamond clip keeping the hair in place. Irritably she fiddled for a moment with that one strand which would never stay where it was placed. At last she managed to make it stay put, just as Alex tapped on her door.

When she opened it he looked at her with narrowed eyes, a faintly grim expression on his face.

'I'm beginning to wonder if I know you at all,' he

said after a pause during which she had coloured deeply.

She tried to answer lightly, forcing her voice to sound bright. 'I thought you wanted me to seduce Ricky.'

His brows drew together. 'I wouldn't advise it,' he said shortly.

'Isn't he susceptible?' she asked, feeling totally out of character, but afraid of the true nature of her feelings as she stood next to him.

'You wouldn't have any problems there,' he said drily. 'Especially in that dress.'

Deborah closed her door, searched through her purse to make sure she had her key, trying to stop the aching in the pit of her stomach as Alex took her arm and she felt the power of those strong fingers around her. 'You said you brought me to Nice to help you persuade him to join us,' she pointed out.

Close to her ear Alex said softly, 'I want to sign him up, not strangle him ...'

She felt a confused sensation of excitement and alarm, her ears drumming. Somehow she walked along the corridor beside him to the lift, trying to force her breathing to slow. In the lift she stood a foot away from him, her eyes lowered. They walked through the foyer to the car park in silence. Alex opened the door and she quickly slid into the passenger seat before he could touch her to assist her. As he took his own seat she settled, far enough away to make sure his hand did not touch her thigh as he moved.

'Did you ring your mother?' she asked him quickly, as he drove out of the hotel car park.

'Yes.' His eyes moved sideways to her. There was a faint frown on his face. 'The line was appalling. I couldn't hear her very well, but I'm a little worried—she sounded upset about something. I got no sense from her, I hope she isn't ill or in trouble.'

'Perhaps you could go to see her when you've finished your business with Ricky,' Deborah suggested. Her blue eyes were concerned. 'You ought to see her, as you're in the neighbourhood.'

'I promised to be back on Saturday,' he said casually.

'Surely your mother is more important than Magda Gilmore,' she said accusingly.

He shrugged. 'I'll try to ring her from the villa. I doubt if Ricky will mind, and his line may be better. Mother is very temperamental. If her work is going badly she's inclined to be excitable.'

'You're far too casual about her,' she said angrily. 'If she lives alone, miles from anywhere, she's probably lonely.'

He gave a short laugh. 'Not my mother! Anyway, she has lots of friends in the next village. Once a week she plays chess with the old village priest, and she visits some old woman who lives there, too; a rather tart old woman, I thought, when I met her, but they get on like a house on fire.'

'Your mother is English, isn't she?' she asked, frowning.

'Of course she is, but she's lived there for years. She isn't lonely. In fact, she left England after my father died because she hated socialising. She likes a quiet life.'

They turned into the drive of Ricky Winter's villa some ten minutes later, through electronically operated gates controlled from the house, their tyres crunching over the silvery gravel until they halted before the house. Isolated behind high walls, in a quiet, exclusive area of Nice, the villa lay among beautifully maintained gardens which were just visible by the soft light flooding from the terrace which ran all the way along the front of the building. A line of cypress trees made an oblong of shadow on one side. Lawns and dark shrubs occupied the main part of the garden. The sky was darkening to the soft purple of a plum. Stars pierced it at intervals, occasionally fading as the glow of an approaching aircraft lit the dark. From a long way off they could hear the sad murmur of the sea.

Ricky was quite different tonight. He had chosen to wear formal evening clothes, his white shirt lacily frilled, the smooth black velvet of his suit making him even thinner and emphasising the shade of his white blond hair. He looked older, less brash, better looking, and as his eyes swept over her the admiration in them was unmistakable.

He bent his head to kiss Deborah's hand, taking her by surprise, and gave her a little grin. 'When in France do as the French do,' he suggested mockingly.

She flickered a glance at Alex. There was a polite movement on his hard mouth, the pretence of a smile, but no warmth in the grey eyes.

The room into which Ricky took them was thirty feet long, the shining woodblock floors reflecting bowls of scented spring flowers which illuminated the room with beauty, the cool white and green of the colour scheme carried through in every object; soft white leather upholstery, floor-length green curtains, lampshades and cushions.

'What a lovely room,' she said, admiring some cold green jade elephants standing along the stone fireplace. 'These are beautiful!'

Ricky moved to a table. 'What will you drink?'

'Gin and tonic,' she said. 'Thank you.'

'Whisky,' Alex said briefly, sinking into a corner of the long couch, his dark sleeve resting along the leather. Ricky joined them, handing them glasses. 'Sit down, Deborah,' he said, his ludicrously long dark lashes glinting at her. She hestitantly sat down on the couch, at the other end from Alex, aware of the long stare he gave her, the lingering way his hard eyes moved over her body and fixed on the slender legs. Crossing them, she sipped her drink. Ricky moved back to them, his glass in his hand, grinned at Alex and said, 'Bags I be Piggy in the Middle.' He sat down between them, his velvet thigh close to her leg, and tilted his glass, smiling at her. 'Cheers ...'

Nervously she looked at the paintings hanging against his white walls. 'You seem to like landscapes.'

'Yeah, I do,' he said casually. 'I bought all these in Paris—they're all French. I like the French landscape.'

'They fit in nicely with your colour scheme too,' said Alex rather tartly. Over the back of the couch Deborah looked at him indignantly. He would ruin any chance of acquiring Ricky for the firm if he made digs at him like that. His eyes met her accusing glance wryly.

'That's not why I bought them,' Ricky said, with touchy irritation. 'I like them.'

Alex swallowed the rest of his amber drink and stood up. 'Would you mind if I made an important local phone call, Ricky? I won't take five minutes.'

'Help yourself,' Ricky invited at once pleasantly. 'Take it in my bedroom.'

'It isn't private,' said Alex, moving across the room to a white telephone which occupied a niche at the further end of the lounge.

'Pity,' Ricky said, lowering his voice, swivelling to face Deborah. 'Two's company, and I could do without him for a while.'

Conscious, although she did not look round, of Alex's watchful gaze while he tried to get his number, she smiled into Ricky's green eyes. 'Don't you miss England now and then?'

'Too busy,' he said, shrugging. 'How long have you worked for Alex?'

They talked about the firm, and then about the

music world in general, until she had an opportunity to ask naturally, 'Is it true you've quarrelled with Russ Wolf?'

He gave her an understanding, teasing smile. 'Yeah, he's a rat, and I've been waiting for the chance to get out of my contract with him for a long time. I signed for seven years. He wants me to renew, but he can whistle.' The shrewd green eyes smiled at her. 'None of which is news to you, darling, or Alex wouldn't be over here.'

She admitted as much with her laughter. 'Alex admires your work very much. He thinks we could help you a good deal ...' She began to outline Alex's ideas of his future to him and he listened, watching her face closely, occasionally asking her quick, shrewd questions.

Ricky was under no illusions about his worth, she realised. His brash conceit was based on years of adulation by the public, and he would not be an easy young man to work with unless one understood him.

Under that glossy exterior, though, he was sharply intelligent, a tough, frank young man who believed in himself and understood his own ability. The sexual conceit he advertised was, she suspected, more for public consumption than from any particular leaning of his own. No doubt fans had pursued him for years. He knew he had, as he said bluntly, the knack of pulling the birds, but he told her with a grin that it was his success in music which was responsible rather than his own looks.

'But you're very good-looking,' she said thoughtfully, looking at him with the eyes of a teenage girl. To young females he must seem exciting, a rough, iconoclastic hero without inhibitions or boundaries. Alex had something of the same appeal to the women who fell for him. They both exuded sex appeal and the allure of the anti-hero.

He grinned at her, leaning over to trail one finger over the parted softness of her mouth. 'You aren't so dusty yourself, darling.'

Behind his shoulder she met Alex's narrowed eyes and drew back. Politely, she asked, 'Did you get through?'

His brow was troubled. 'No reply,' he said. 'I've tried several times. I thought the phone must be out of order, but the operator told me it was ringing and getting no reply. I can't understand it. Mother never goes out in the evening.'

'She's off with her boy-friend, old darling,' Ricky said lightly.

Alex shrugged. 'I'll try again tomorrow.'

Ricky's housekeeper announced dinner a few seconds later and they moved through to the dining-room, Alex moving a few yards in front of Ricky and Deborah, who were, to her amusement, hand in hand, although Ricky's deftness in accomplishing this had taken her by surprise.

The meal was excellent, superbly cooked and served by flickering candlelight, around a table sufficiently large to leave them all comfortably apart yet small enough to be intimate. Deborah had difficulty in persuading Ricky that she could not cope with the amount of wine he pressed upon her. Whenever she took her eyes off her glass he refilled it. He was a lively, entertaining host, refusing to discuss business while they ate, and talking instead about France, painting, cars and the large family he had left behind in England. 'I wanted them to come over here to live, but my mum wouldn't budge. A creature of habit, my old mum.' He put his hand over Deborah's silken thigh. 'She'd like you, darling. My old mum always did like lady-like girls. She's keen on good manners, my mum.'

Giving him a little smile, she discreetly moved his

hand back to his lap. 'She sounds very nice,' she said warmly. 'I hope she slapped you when you were naughty.'

His green eyes danced. 'Just like windmills, her hands.'

'I expect you needed it,' she said. 'It's probably a family characteristic.'

Ricky laughed delightedly. 'Hey, I like it!' He looked at her through those dark lashes. 'I like you, too, darling. I could have done with you when I was on the road. God, one-night stands take it out of you. I got so tired I could hardly keep my eyes open. We used to sleep in the van on the way to our next gig, and we needed a few laughs to stop us going nuts.'

'How did you start in the business?' she asked, rising as they moved back to the long lounge to drink their coffee. The wine had made her faintly muzzy and the air seemed stuffy and hot. She felt a strong inclination to lie back against the cushions of the couch and drowsily close her eyes. Accepting black coffee, she sipped it in the hope that it would help her to stay awake.

Eagerly Ricky plunged into a clearly nostalgic tale of his first days in the profession, then insisted on getting his guitar in order to play her the first tune he ever wrote. Alone with Alex during his absence, Deborah leaned back thankfully, her lids drooping.

'Enjoying yourself?' Alex asked her sardonically.

Forcing her eyes open, she looked at him dazedly. 'Very much,' she murmured.

'Like me to leave?' he asked bitingly.

She stared. 'What?'

'You've been giving him the green light all evening. I've no doubt he expects you to stay when I leave,' he said coldly.

She flushed hotly. 'Oh, shut up! You asked me to

be nice to him. Now you're turning it into something vile.'

The door opened before he could answer and Ricky came back with his guitar. He posed, laughing, more than a little drunk. His pale hair was attractively disarranged, he had unbuttoned his black velvet jacket and the two top buttons of his frilled shirt, his bow tie discarded. 'Spanish, see?' he explained, his long hands caressing the smoothly polished wood with loving care. 'I had it made for me over there. I learnt to play classical guitar first, now I play electric, because it sells better. This is a lovely instrument. Listen to this tone ...' He stood easily, one foot on the low velvet footstool he obviously kept for the purpose, and played a gentle, rather sad little melody which Deborah found very pleasant. It was nothing like the music he usually played, which was moody and full of rhythmic savagery, all chords and crashing sound.

'That's lovely,' she told him sincerely. 'I like it better than your usual material.'

He shrugged. 'The commercial stuff sells better. Bubble gum music ... plastic and forgettable. Just a few people like my early stuff.'

'Did you ever record them?' she asked.

He shook his head. 'Russ didn't go for them.'

She looked at Alex. 'What do you think?'

Ricky looked at Alex, too, his green glance defiant. 'He won't like them any more than Russ did.'

'You're wrong,' Alex said crisply. 'Have you got many like that?'

Ricky sat down on the arm of the couch and looked at him, narrow-eyed. 'Soft soap or for real?'

'I never risk hard cash on soft soap,' said Alex. 'If you can come up with a tape full of stuff like that I think we could sell it.'

Ricky's flush deepened. The talk became serious.

Discreetly, Deborah slipped into the background, letting Alex lead the discussion. He negotiated toughly, but smoothly, and it was a pleasure to watch him at the job. He knew exactly what he was doing when he performed this function, she thought. He and Ricky fenced tirelessly, each trying to strike the best bargain, but although he badly wanted Ricky on his list Alex showed no sign of weakness or bluff, countering all Ricky's demands and refusals until at last they came to a hard-fought agreement.

'Shake on it?' Alex asked him with a smile, and they firmly shook hands. 'I'll let you have the agreement when it's drawn up.'

'I'll fly over to London to sign,' Ricky promised. He slanted a wicked green glance at Deborah. 'Have lunch with me then, darling?'

'Thank you,' she smiled, 'I'd love to.'

Alex stood up abruptly. 'I'm afraid we'll have to be going now. It must be nearly midnight, and we have a plane to catch tomorrow.'

Ricky had a sullen glint in his eyes as he said, 'I thought we were having another session tomorrow morning? Nice by my pool. Deb can swim while we chat, then I'll have something sexy to look at while I talk.'

'I'm sure Deborah would enjoy that,' said Alex, his tone sardonic. 'Our plane leaves in the afternoon, so we'll see you tomorrow.'

Ricky cheered up, his wide mouth curving. 'Fine,' he said. He walked with them to the door, halting Deborah as he stood aside to let Alex move outside. Into her ear, he said softly, 'Cards on the table, honey. You Alex's property?'

She flushed. 'No!' Her voice was sharp.

'Fine,' he said again, with satisfaction. 'I got an idea you might be.'

DUEL OF DESIRE

She said goodnight and joined Alex. Ricky waved as the car moved off down the drive, then the gates smoothly swung open and they spun out into the road. Alex drove in total silence, his profile unreadable in the dark interior of the car. Deborah felt oddly nervous. Somehow she expected some barbed remarks. His attitude all evening had been puzzlingly difficult to read. He had asked her to be nice to Ricky, yet he had sniped at her all the time whenever he spoke to her. Could he be sexually jealous? Yet if he resented it whenever she was friendly to another man ... She caught herself up angrily. Sexually jealous ... the phrase disturbed her. She wished it had not entered her mind.

When they arrived at the hotel she blinked as her eyes became accustomed to the bright lights, following Alex to the desk to collect their keys. The terse silence persisted as they went upstairs in the lift, and he walked past her to his own room without even saying goodnight. Angrily she let herself into her room and went straight into the bathroom. Bolting the door on his side, she stripped and showered, then changed into her brief green lace nightgown.

Her room was so stuffy that she opened the french windows. Drawn by the cool air and the illuminated promenade she moved out on to the balcony and leaned on the rail, breathing in the fresh night fragrance. Her head was still heavy after all that wine. She stared at the dark sea, remembering the raft swinging gently under her shoulders as Alex forced her to admit her own need for his lovemaking. She closed her eyes, groaning soundlessly. When she went back to London she must tell Robin she could never marry him. Knowing as she did now how badly she had wanted Alex to touch her she knew she must not, could not, marry Robin. It would cheat him. There would be no reality in the vows they exchanged. How could she swear fidelity when she had betrayed her own intelligence by weakening under Alex's attack? But she must also leave the firm. She had to get away from Alex; the effect he had on her was disastrous. If she stayed within his ambiance one day he might succeed in persuading her to drift into an affair with him. She no longer trusted her own strength of mind where he was concerned. She had been sure she could resist him, but it had been the confidence of folly.

She was so involved in her thoughts that she did not hear the movements behind her until Alex was a few feet away. Then she spun, eyes wide. Like herself, he had showered. His dark hair was damp. He wore a short white towelling dressing-gown, and beneath it his legs were bare.

The silvery eyes moved probingly over her. She had not even thought to put on a negligee, since she had intended to go to bed until drawn out by the wine-sweet air of the night. The thin lace of her nightgown fluttered in the wind, revealing the thin side slits which ran from the hem to the hip. Shivering, more from his inspection than from the wind, she said, 'It ... it's getting cold. I think I'll go in ...'

He moved into her path silently as she moved to go inside. The brooding darkness of his eyes transfixed her like a moth fascinated by fire. She fought in her mind to escape him, but her body was swept by sensations against which she had fought for too long. With the rush of a bursting dam, the flood of desire drowned her mind.

Past concealment, evasion, rejection, she waited helplessly as he lowered his face towards her. 'I've been waiting all evening for this,' he said harshly, his mouth closing over her lips.

They kissed desperately, her arms closing around the back of his head to pull him nearer, her slender, half-naked body shuddering in his arms. He broke off the kiss to ask roughly, 'You've been waiting too, haven't you, Deb?'

'Yes,' she admitted in bitter weakness. She had talked, smiled, performed her part in the social minuet of the evening with one thought at the back of her mind, the memory of the moments out on the raft. Her light flirtation with Ricky had been a deliberate attempt to force down more dangerous thoughts. She had told herself again and again she would not allow Alex to touch her again—yet now she could no more resist him than she could fight against herself. The sensuality against which she had fought for years had the upper hand. She had no power or desire to halt or control the hunger which was driving her.

He picked her up in his arms as if she were a child, the frail lace blown upwards to expose her naked thighs. Walking through the open french windows into her bedroom, he laid her down on to the bed. She was hot, yet shivering, as if she had a fever, looking up at him as he lay down beside her with passion-glazed blue eyes.

Staring at her with brooding savagery, he said, 'All evening I've wanted to touch you, to be alone with you, and I had to watch while you smiled at that boy and let him flatter you and flirt with you. The little swine even put his hand on your leg, and you let him. Do you think I didn't know what was going on?'

'You brought me here to be nice to him,' she said, looking at him through her lashes, her senses stirring at the obvious jealousy in his face and voice.

'You've handled boys like him a dozen times before,' he said irritably. 'And you've kept them at a distance while you played them along. Tonight you were deliberately encouraging that boy.' His eyes blazed. 'I was the real target, wasn't I? You knew damned well what it was doing to me to watch you with him.'

'I was pleasant to him,' she retorted, angered by the accusation. 'That was what you wanted, wasn't it? In the past you've accused me of being too unbending with clients. You hinted that you wanted me to be as accommodating with our male artists as you've always been with the female ones ...'

He tensed and stared down into her eyes. 'Jealous, Deb?' The question was uttered on a new note which sent shivers down her spine. She read the eagerness in his voice, the pulsating triumph, and she sat up angrily.

'No,' she denied. 'Just contemptuous of your methods in business, Alex. Why should I be jealous? There's little value in something which so many others have been offered.'

The insult made him rigid for a few seconds, and an ugly smile lifted his mouth. Deborah felt a tremor of fear as the menace in his eyes deepened, but before she could move away he had pushed her backwards on to the bed, his hands encompassing the warmth of her half-exposed breasts. An ache grew strongly inside her. His fingers tightened, hurting her ruthlessly. She moaned, her head moving from side to side in bitter protest. Alex pulled down the thin straps and caressed her slowly. Beneath the skin of his palms her nipples hardened. She twisted restlessly, her eyes shut. No man had ever touched her like this before. The poignant, terrifying sweetness was new to her, and she struggled to reach the lost ability to deny him.

Gasping for breath, she pushed away the hard intrusive hands, surprised when he did not stop her. Opening her eyes, she tensed in terror as she realised he was untying the belt of his dressing-gown.

'No!' she said fiercely.

'You want me,' he said between his teeth. 'You've admitted it. We're not playing games, Deb—this is real.

Grow up, for God's sake. Ever since this afternoon I've been waiting for this moment. I won't let you stop me.'

'I must have been mad,' she said bitterly. 'It was just an impulse, a momentary weakness. I don't want to go to bed with you, Alex. I drank too much wine. It was the wine ...'

'It wasn't the wine,' he said tersely. 'It was this.' She struggled as his body arched over her, but she was incapable of fighting against the strength with which he subdued her, and his mouth took her lips with savage ferocity, his body crushing her back against the bed. Imprisoned by the hard, muscled thighs, she twisted and turned in her attempts to escape, tasting the salt tang of her own blood on her tongue as his mouth bruised her lips against her teeth in an effort to part them. She could fight against that savage mouth, but she was helpless to fight against her own body as it slowly quivered under his exploring hands. Dizzy waves of desire mounted to her head. Gradually her resistance ceased. As Alex felt the change, his kiss altered to become gently seductive. With a groan her lips parted at last, and his tongue softly touched the torn inner softness.

'I'm sorry I hurt you,' he whispered softly against her mouth. 'I don't want to hurt you, Deb. But don't fight me. Stop pretending. You want it as much as I do ...'

'Oh, Alex,' she groaned, her voice carrying its own message of total surrender. Her hands moved against him, caressing the rough skin of his chest, the dark hair prickling the palms, sending erotic signals down her spine.

His chest rose and fell rapidly under her touch. He watched her, breathing hard. Pushing back the loose blonde hair from her face, his fingers searched the hollows beneath her ears, her neck, her heated nape.

His hand curved round the back of her head in a sudden movement of possession, pushing her face into his chest. Under her hot cheek the coolness of his skin was agony and delight. Breathing fiercely, she kissed him, her mouth tasting the rough maleness of his skin for the first time. Muffled against his chest, burning and inescapable, she groaned, 'Oh, Alex, I want you ...'

She felt as well as heard the hoarse sound he made. He pulled her head back and lowered his own, their mouths clinging, filled with a driving physical need which beat through her veins like fire, turning her body into helpless fluidity. She was only conscious of a need to please and satisfy him. He held her body between his roving hands and she made no effort to stop him, shuddering with pleasure under the kiss which seemed to last endlessly, as though in itself it were an act of possession.

I'm in love, she thought, in the distant recess of her mind. I love him. His presence in a room had always made her more aware than she had dared admit. He had gradually filled every corner of her heart without her either being able to stop it or admit it. Her driving need to give herself to him, to throw away years of firm principle, was the ultimate expression of a love which, like an unwanted weed, had thrived on stony soil, in spite of her constant attempts to unroot it, deny it, drive it away. Now in the miracle of desire it flowered, and she stood speechless before that splendour, recognising at last that the powerful unwanted plant was love itself.

Reluctantly Alex lifted his mouth, looking at her with eyes which moved over her hungrily. 'I swear I won't hurt you, Deb,' he said thickly. 'Oh, God, you drive me mad. For years you've been under my skin, tormenting me. I've wanted to make love to you for so long ...'

'Tell me you love me, Alex,' she whispered eagerly, her blue eyes glazed with passion.

He was still for a moment. A frown twisted his face. 'Oh, Deb, don't use words like that. They just confuse the issue. Love is a word people use to describe their sexual needs. It's the pretty wrapping women prefer ... I want us to be honest. I'm a man and I want you. It's as simple as that.'

A chill sensation feathered over her skin. She stared at him, her eyes cooling. 'Then any woman would do.'

'No,' he said harshly, his silvery eyes flickering over the slender body he had just caressed with such passion. 'It has to be you. Celibacy has never interested me, you know that. I've never hidden my affairs from you. But for a long time now I haven't been able to want anyone else. I haven't slept with anyone for months.'

She felt a sharp stab of triumph and joy at the admission. 'Not even Sammy Starr?' she asked, half teasingly, half gladly.

He shook his head. 'Sammy? I've told you, there's been no one. Oh, I've taken girls out, danced with them, even taken them to my flat. But I couldn't raise a flicker of desire. You came between me and every damned one of them.' Jaggedly he said, 'At times I almost hated you for what you were doing to me. You don't know how many times in the office I had to fight down a need to touch you. Every time you came near me I could think of nothing else.'

She had known. She had fought the same battle, and despite her desire to pretend she did not know how he felt she had been conscious of his sexual awareness of her every minute of the day. She was aware of it now, burning within both of them, a need so urgent it was painful.

Alex's face filled with harshness. 'I want you, but I won't lie to you, and say foolish, easy nonsense like "I love you". A man is an animal. My need for you is a sexual drive so strong it's kept me awake at night, especially since you started going out with Robin. That finished me. I've never been jealous before in my life, but I was then ...' His eyes burned down at her resentfully. 'Enjoy your little triumph, Deb. I began to detest poor inoffensive Robin, and I was half demented at the thought that he was doing to you what I wanted to do.'

'Oh, Alex,' she sighed, pain and anguish filling her. 'You'd better go. You're honest, I have to admit that, but your view of life is so alien to me that we might be from different planets. You see sex as an appetite to be relieved. I can't see it like that.'

'But you want me,' he said, unanswerably, and his eyes demanded her submission. 'What do you expect me to say? Can't you see we both need it?' His hands possessively moved over her, his fingers trembling. 'Feel it, Deb. Feel the way I want you, and admit you want me, too.'

'I admit it,' she said quietly. His face flooded with triumph. 'How many other women have you wanted, Alex?' His expression changed, a brooding look came into his features. 'I doubt if you even know how many there've been. I'm not going to become one of your trophies, a toy you play with for a while, then throw away.'

'This time it's different,' he said huskily. 'I've never wanted anyone as much as I want you.'

'You've never had to wait before, have you, Alex?' she asked drily. 'I suspect that the fact that I was out of your reach has made you frantic to get me. Well, I'm still out of your reach, Alex. I suppose you could always rape me, but you wouldn't enjoy that much, would you? And I'll never say yes to you again.'

He ran his hands through his hair roughly, staring

at her. His eyes were leaping with tormented feeling, his jaw tense as though he was suffering acute pain. She looked back at him calmly.

'You've said no often enough before,' he said, as though thinking to himself. 'But just now I know damned well I almost had you.'

'Almost,' she admitted wryly. 'But you'll never get so close again, Alex.'

Believing the certainty in her voice, he breathed harshly. 'All right, you win. I'll marry you. I've been in business for too long not to know that there are some things which you have to have, even when you know damned well the price is too high.'

Just for a few seconds joy pierced her, but she knew his offer was not what she wanted. Quietly she said, 'Alex, you can't marry me just to get me into bed with you.'

'No man marries for any other reason,' he said cynically. 'Women marry to get security for life. Men marry only because they're trapped.'

'As you are?' she asked softly.

He looked at her angrily, eyes hardening, then a groan came from him. 'Yes,' he admitted. 'It's taken you four years, Deb, but I'm caught in your silken little web and eager to be devoured.'

'I'm not a female spider, Alex,' she said, shaking her head. 'You're free to go, I assure you.'

He smiled mirthlessly. 'Like hell I'm free! You've had me in a corner for months waiting for me to admit I was beaten. I'm past caring what price I have to pay to get you.'

'You like things straightforward and simple,' she said calmly. 'I'll lay it on the line for you. I refuse to go to bed with you and I refuse to marry you. Is that clear enough for you?'

She watched the dark colour flush up under his skin.

His nostrils flared in rage. She met his incredulous, angry gaze without flinching. It was easier to face his anger than his pain. She was aching with love for him even as she refused him, but she knew she could not marry him on such terms.

He swore so savagely she flinched at last. 'My God, you little bitch, I could strangle you!' His mouth snarled savagely at her. 'Is this your idea of a joke? You deliberately got me to admit I wanted you enough to marry you so that you could have the triumph of turning me down!' His face contorted with bitterness. 'Are you looking forward to spreading the story around? God, beaten by a girl who wouldn't even go to bed ... it would be the joke of the year in the business, wouldn't it? You'll make me the laughing-stock of London ...' Flame invaded his eyes. Deborah suddenly saw a new look on his features, a bitter menace and hostility mingling with tormented desire. 'Let's see if you still want to tell the joke with a different ending,' he said thickly.

She understood what he intended to do even before he began to kiss her again, uncaring now if he hurt her, wanting to hurt her, his hands savagely insulting as he handled her body. The few frail strips of lace between the nakedness of their bodies were torn away, and Alex's mouth burned on her skin with violent insistence. She forced herself to lie limply and unresponsively beneath him, although she was driven almost to madness by uncontrollable response to the hunger of his lovemaking. She could hear his heart pounding, the raggedness of his breathing as he moved against her. He was shaking with bitterness and desire, an explosive mixture, wanting to crush her into submission, bruising her white body as though his threat to kill her were not idle.

Gradually he stiffened and drew away, staring at her with naked hatred in his eyes.

'I can't even take you by force, can I?' he asked harshly. 'You're right—I can't make love to a cold bitch like you. I could take you if you fought me, but it's like making love to a statue.'

'I think you'd better go, Alex,' she said quietly, drawing on years of pretending indifference to him, although it was agony to see that look on his face.

His mouth curved in an ugly sneer. 'I suppose you're going to marry Robin, after all. Has it occurred to you that I could give you more material comfort than he can? I'm not a dependable, virtuous little robot like him, of course. You'd have to put up with my disgusting desires once in a while ... but I'm a damned sight richer.'

'I'm not interested in your money,' she said, stung. 'I just want to be happy. Happiness is a basic human need, as strong as the need for sex, Alex. You may never have needed it, but the rest of us do. Robin may not be as rich or as sexy as you are, but marriage to him would be infinitely preferable to marriage to you.' To you when I know you don't love me, she thought in anguish. Hell would be sweeter than that.

Alex stared down at her and his face slowly drained of colour. Cruel lines of hatred carved themselves in the white stone of his face. She was shocked and alarmed by the expression in the grey eyes. 'You little bitch,' he said hoarsely. Standing up, he tied his dressing-gown with a jerk of hands that shook, sent a comprehensive glance of savage dismissal over her body, and walked unsteadily out of the room.

Deborah lay, long-damned tears spilling down her pale face. The love she had recognised and admitted after so painful a struggle had proved full of anguish. It would have been so easy to marry Alex. At least she would have had something. Perhaps she should have accepted the desire he offered her, given him what he wanted, but she knew the after-taste of the honey of passion would have been bitter in her mouth. She loved him and she wanted him desperately, but marriage between them would have been hell on earth for her, knowing he would never love her.

CHAPTER FIVE

It was strange to sleep so deeply when her mind was so disturbed, but her mental and physical exhaustion was such that she fell soon afterwards into bottomless sleep, her body curled on its side, one hand beneath her cheek, in the attitude of a weary child. She awoke with a start, hearing a movement, and her lids reluctantly raised themselves in the face of strong sunlight. Against the open french windows, his body taut, Alex was standing staring at her. For a moment they looked at each other in silence. From complete relaxation Deborah felt herself plunge into breathless awareness. His face was an expressionless mask. All traces of the savagery he had shown last night were gone.

'I was beginning to wonder if you would ever wake up,' he said flatly.

She stretched, her arms lifted over her head. Under her lowered lashes she saw the grey eyes move swiftly over her as the movement outlined her body under the sheet covering her. 'What time is it?' she asked casually.

'Eleven o'clock,' he said tersely, turning away, his hands thrust down into the back pockets of his jeans. He was wearing a black strawcloth shirt through which she could see the silver medallion Sammy had given him.

She was astonished. 'As late as that? Why didn't you knock hours ago?'

'I did,' he said grimly, 'but there was no reply.' His profile was taut. 'So in the end I came round to see ...' He broke off whatever he had been about to say. Curiously, Deborah probed the unyielding profile.

'See what?' she asked lightly.

He turned to her, his eyes icy. 'For God's sake! I thought...' He seemed unable to put it into words.

She frowned, puzzled. 'Thought...?' Her eyes widened. 'What did you think, Alex? That I'd gone?'

He bit out the words savagely. 'That, or... how did I know? There wasn't a sound from you, and the desk clerk told me you hadn't checked out. Your key wasn't down there, so you couldn't have gone out. About a hundred different possibilities existed.'

'Such as what?' she asked, smiling with amusement.

He did not look amused. 'You might be sick,' he said grimly. 'Or worse.'

Deborah's blue eyes watched him through the veil of her lashes. 'Did you think I might be dead, Alex?' The question was softly teasing.

He turned towards the french windows. 'Get up and we'll go round to see Ricky,' he said. 'He rang an hour ago to find out why we weren't there. You've got him mesmerised, he can't wait to see you again.'

She asked his retreating back, 'You didn't think I might have committed suicide, Alex?' Her tone was as smooth as silk.

'If you ever feel like that I'll save you the trouble,' he said bitterly. 'Sooner or later someone's going to wring your neck, anyway.'

She laughed. He went out, slamming the french window shut behind him so that the glass shivered and the curtains blew back into the room.

He might be furious, she thought, walking into the bathroom, but he could not disguise the fact that anxiety had run beneath his anger.

She dressed and joined him ten minutes later. 'What about breakfast?' he asked her curtly. 'I had mine hours ago.'

'I'm not hungry,' she said truthfully. 'But I would like some coffee.'

'I'm sure Ricky will provide some, then,' he said unpleasantly.

They drove to the villa in silence. This morning, in bright sunlight, it slept in graceful peace, the lawns so smooth they did not look real, the brilliant colours of the spring flowers still carrying dew at their centres. A gardener in a straw hat was moving about, hosing the borders, his shoulders damp with perspiration. Ricky met them, sulkily demanding of Deborah why she was so late. She apologised, explaining that she had overslept, and he looked sideways at Alex, his frown making it clear he suspected them of having been together all night.

Alex's jaw clenched. 'Are we going to swim?' he asked tersely.

'Come round to the pool,' said Ricky, still sullen. He was wearing a brief white pair of trunks, slung low on the hip, his body smoothly golden from the sun. Against his brown body his white hair looked even more fantastic.

Alex moved away rapidly and they walked after him. Ricky gave Deborah a reproachful look. 'You said you weren't his girl,' he accused.

'I overslept because I was tired,' she said softly. 'I've never slept with Alex. Sorry to disillusion you, but some of us still have old-fashioned values. If I slept with someone it would be because I loved him. Alex isn't my lover.'

His eyes searched her face, then he grinned. 'What are you, a museum piece? I thought that sort of attitude went out with elastic-sided boots?'

She shrugged. 'You may be right.'

He grimaced. 'Marriage or nothing, eh?'

Her eyes lowered. Once she might have said that, but

now she knew that had Alex said he loved her she would not have sent him away. Her own love for him was too strong. 'Love or nothing,' she said huskily. 'Sex without it is as meaningless as food when one has no appetite.'

Ricky frowned, his thin face bothered. 'My mum would agree with you, but I never expected to find another woman who talked like that.'

She laughed. 'I should find yourself one, Ricky.'

They reached the pool, strolling at a slow pace. Alex had already changed and was standing on the smooth white tiles, staring into the artificially blue water. Ricky paused, a few feet from him, and looked at her wickedly. 'I've just found one, haven't I?'

She flushed, looking at him with surprise. 'I meant ...' she began, and he said teasingly, 'I know what you meant, darling.'

Alex glanced over his shoulder at them, his eyes chips of grey ice.

'I'll change,' Deborah said hurriedly, ducking into the small building beside the pool.

When she emerged a while later both men were in the water, tossing a red beach-ball from one to the other. She dived into the pool, her slender body cutting the water cleanly. She swam the length of the pool slowly, then trod water, watching as the men continued playing their game. 'Come and play,' Ricky invited.

She shook her head, her wet hair flicking across her shoulders. For a while she lazed, drifting on the water, then she climbed out and lay down on a low blue lounger, staring at the incredible blue sky.

A few moments later the two men joined her. Alex sat down under a red umbrella, beside a white table, and poured himself a glass of lemonade. Ricky took the lounger adjacent to hers and grinned at her. 'Like a drink now?'

'She hasn't had any breakfast,' said Alex. 'I suppose there's no chance of some coffee?'

'No,' Deborah said quickly. 'It's nearly lunchtime now. It doesn't matter.'

'Sure?' Ricky asked. 'My housekeeper could bring you some croissants and coffee, you know.'

'I'm certain,' she said.

'You're having lunch here, aren't you?' Ricky asked.

She glanced at Alex, who surveyed her unsmilingly. 'Why, thank you,' he said pleasantly, but his expression was far from pleasant. 'We've still got a lot to talk about, Ricky. This is very enjoyable, but we have to talk some time.'

'Yeah,' said Ricky, leaning back, his slim shoulders settling against the lounger. 'Later...' His hand moved and trailed over her naked thigh. 'Are you awake, sleeping beauty?'

Deborah opened her eyes to smile at him. 'Just about. This sunshine is soporific.'

'Nice word,' he said mockingly. 'What does it mean?'

'It makes me feel sleepy,' she said, laughing.

'It certainly doesn't describe you, then,' he said, uncaring of Alex's listening presence. 'You don't affect me like that at all.'

She wrinkled her nose at him. In the past such a remark from a young man might have irritated her, but she treated it lightly now. Her realisation that she loved Alex had given the world a new brightness, freeing her from many of her cherished inhibitions. She felt laughter bubbling inside her chest. Happiness seemed to course in her blood. It was curious that despite her pain that Alex could not return the love she felt, she was so euphoric in his presence. Her nerves were newly sensitised. Everything seemed to be new to her. Her eyes saw the world with fresh clarity. Smiles of pure delight curved her mouth. She felt free, free of the old longing for affection and security, the obsessive pattern-making which had made her arrange everything in her life so neatly. There was no room for anything inside her but her love for Alex now. It had changed everything.

Ricky moved restlessly. 'How about another swim?' he asked her.

She cheerfully got up and they entered the water again. For some time they swam side by side, then played with the beach-ball. Ricky teased her about her poor aim, and Deborah flung the ball straight at him, catching him in the chest so that he slid down into the water. Coughing, he came up and pursued her for vengeance, while she laughed and fled, climbing out of the pool, dripping.

Alex looked coldly at her as she sank down on the lounger. Ricky stood over her, breathing fast, his hands on his hips. Shaking back his wet blond hair he said in mock wrath, 'I'll owe you for that, darling.'

'Can we talk now?' Alex asked him abruptly.

Ricky groaned. 'Persistent devil, aren't you? Okay, fire ahead.'

They talked for almost an hour, sitting around the table, the sunshine glinting off the blue water, the fragrance of the flowers which surrounded the pool in white tubs, scenting the warm air. Ricky looked suddenly at his watch and made a face. 'Madame will be waiting for us to go in to lunch.' He jumped up. 'We'll change first, Alex.'

While the two men changed Deborah lay with eyes closed, enjoying the silence and warmth of the morning. The sun was growing stronger as the day wore on, but she enjoyed the feel of it as it soaked into her skin, bringing a flush to it. When she heard a step she lazily opened her eyes, and her heart hammered as her gaze encountered Alex's grey eyes. They were moving lingeringly over her slender body. The black bikini left so little to the imagination that it merely drew attention to the swell of her white breasts, the flatness of her stomach, the long curve of her hips and thighs. She felt her breasts grow heavy under his gaze, the nipples tauten so that they were visible under the silken cloth.

Ricky came out of the changing-room, apparently oblivious of the atmosphere between them. Cheerfully he said, 'I'll run in and tell Madame we're on our way. Come along when you're ready, Deb.'

He vanished at a graceful lope, his boy's body slim in his white pants and T-shirt. Deborah slid to the floor and turned to go into the changing-room. Alex stood in front of the door, and she looked at him warily.

He moved out of the way abruptly and she passed him. When she came out a few moments later he was walking back towards the house, his dark head erect. Sighing, she followed.

They had a very enjoyable lunch; home-made pâté with crisp golden toast and a small salad, trout au Bretonne, the flesh white and melting, served with deliciously cooked prawns, followed by fresh fruit. Ricky picked at his food. 'I have to watch my diet,' he sighed.

They had a very enjoyable lunch; home-made pâté flower-bordered patio in the sunlight. Ricky kept Deborah amused by his tales of life on the road, the boredom, excitement and lethargy which he had suffered.

'I think you miss it,' she said shrewdly.

He made a face. 'Like I miss a hole in the head.' Then he quirked a grin at her. 'Yeah, maybe I do, too.'

In the middle of the afternoon Alex said coolly, 'We really have to go now, Ricky. Both Deborah and I have important appointments in London tomorrow.

We have to get that plane.'

Ricky was reluctant to let them go. 'Sure you can't stay on?' he asked Deborah pleadingly.

She smiled at him. Despite his aggressive sexuality there was a good deal of the little boy in him, and she felt easy in his company. He talked a lot about sex, but she had not felt any real apprehension about his feelings. He just enjoyed talking about music and his early life to her. Many of the people he met out here in Nice were strangers to the world he had led in London as a young boy. No doubt he felt rootless, alienated.

'When you fly over to London you must come to dinner at my flat,' she said. 'I'll cook you Irish stew to remind you of the old days in digs.'

He laughed. 'Don't forget to put more bones than meat into it, then,' he said. 'I'll take you up on that.'

Ricky accompanied them to their car, waving until they were out of sight. Alex gave her a dry, sideways look. 'He'll be hoping for a lot more than Irish stew,' he said crisply. 'You've never invited one of our clients to your flat before.'

She shrugged. 'Ricky's rather sweet, don't you think?'

'Sweet?' His voice held distaste. 'I wonder if Robin will take the same attitude? Or will his mercenary mind ignore what's going on?'

'Robin isn't mercenary,' she said indignantly.

Alex made a sound of disgust. 'Do you think he doesn't know I've fancied you for years? I've made no secret of the fact.'

She flushed. After a pause she said, 'Yes, Robin thinks ...' Her voice halted in embarrassment.

'He knows,' he said harshly. 'He knows damned well I want you.'

She stared at the white sun-dazzled road. 'But he trusts me,' she said, in deliberate provocation.

Alex's hands tightened on the wheel. The car surged forward, taking a corner at incredible speed. For the rest of the drive they said nothing. Deborah went into her own room and began to pack her case. Alex tapped on the door and came into the room, a frown on his face.

'What's wrong?' she asked, intuitively sensing something was worrying him.

'I've still had no reply from my mother,' he said. 'Look, I think I'll drive over there this afternoon. Our ticket is for the six o'clock flight, isn't it? I can get there and back before the flight leaves. If Mother isn't at the cottage I'll go into the village and see if anyone there knows anything.'

Concerned, she asked, 'Would you like me to come with you?' She knew she could not leave him to face possible bad news on his own. His worry about his mother was at least a sign that he could care deeply about another human being, and she could not bear to think of him being faced with anxiety or grief alone.

He looked at her harshly. 'I'm sure you'd rather go back to Ricky's villa and enjoy yourself with him. It will be a dull drive, and it may be a wild goose chase. Mother may be visiting someone.'

Her blue eyes were gentle. 'Do you want me to come or not, Alex?' she asked him steadily.

He made an irritable face. 'Come if you like,' he said indifferently. 'We'll check out of the hotel when we get back. Leave the rest of your packing until later.'

They drove out of Nice at a fast speed, passing upwards through rough mountain countryside, the road steep and busy with traffic. Alex seemed to have little to say to her. Once or twice he said something about the countryside, but otherwise they went on in silence, each cocooned in their own thoughts.

The countryside flattened. Cypress trees made a dark

shade at the side of the road. Fields ran on either side. They had been driving for half an hour when the sky began to cloud over and rain began to fall, gently at first, and then in a heavy downpour which forced Alex to slow to a crawl, his wipers clicking to and fro rapidly to clear the rush of rain from his view.

Ahead of them they could now see that the sky was black. Inky clouds hovered low over the horizon, although behind them they could still see the halcyon blue skies of the coast in the distance.

Alex swore under his breath. 'We're running into a storm,' he said harshly. 'You should have stayed in Nice.'

'I'm not frightened of a little rain,' Deborah shrugged.

'A little!' he snorted disgustedly. 'My God, girl, it's going to get worse before it gets better.'

They turned off the highway a short time later, running along narrow lanes through isolated hamlets until they began to descend a steep road. The storm increased in violence, and on these narrow country roads Alex had to drive with great care. The roads curved crazily, and the state of their surfaces left a good deal to be desired. The car jerked and bounced over ruts and rough surfaces, the sound of the storm outside growing louder and louder.

Deborah rubbed at her side window, peering out. They had closed all the windows and the interior of the car had steamed up. Lightning tore down the black sky, the flash of it making her start violently. She shrank away from the window, her hand automatically reaching for the security of Alex's arm. The sonorous roll of the thunder seemed to be right above them. She was shaken with terror. The sound deafened her. She clutched at Alex instinctively, just as he was taking a bend, and the movement made his arm jerk. The car veered sharply to the wrong side of the road. Luckily they were going at such a slow speed that when they hit a tree the impact merely threw them both forward and made the car bonnet fly upward. Dazed, Deborah sat up, her forehead throbbing from the blow it had received on the dashboard. Alex disentangled himself from the steering wheel, clutching his midriff.

'Alex! Are you hurt?' Anxiously she turned in her seat to face him, her own pain forgotten.

He groaned. 'I'm not dead,' he said grimly. 'But that damned steering wheel was rammed into me hard. I feel as though I'd been kicked in the stomach by a mule.'

She leaned across, worried. Without pausing to think she pushed back his shirt hurriedly and ran her fingers over the bare skin of his midriff, examining it for signs of injury, trying to see how hurt he had been. 'There, does that hurt?' she asked, her fingers pressing into his flesh gently.

'Like hell,' he said, his voice suddenly hoarse.

She looked at him quickly and her heart thudded. His voice and face told her clearly enough that he was not referring to any injury. She pulled her hands away, hot colour sweeping to her hairline.

Unclipping her seat-belt, she opened the car door and scrambled out. The rain poured down, rapidly saturating her clothes and flattening her hair to her temples. Alex joined her, apparently in control of his face once more, his expression grim as he surveyed the bonnet of the car. He slammed the bonnet down, making a wry face.

'We've made a mess of the radiator,' he said.

'I'm sorry,' she stammered. 'It was my fault.'

He shrugged. Rain ran down his face and soaked through his shirt, making it cling to his body so closely she could see every muscle clearly outlined, as though he were naked. 'At least we're alive,' he said. 'All I hope is that we can start the car again. We're about a mile from my mother's cottage and there's no village for four miles back. The nearest garage is about seven miles off.'

They got back into the car. 'Keep your fingers crossed,' he said, starting the ignition. Astonishingly, it sprang to life at the second attempt, and he carefully reversed back from the tree. They started to drive around the corner and emerged on to a flat narrow road bordered on one side by trees through which she could just see a river bank. On the other ran orchards whose blossom-covered branches tossed wildly to and fro in the wind.

Alex sighed with relief, driving a little faster. The rain still ran in rivers across their windscreen. The sky was almost as dark as if it were night. But they were at least able to drive. He gave Deborah a smile of pure relief. 'Another five minutes and we should see Mother's cottage. It's the only building for miles.'

'It must be a beautiful spot when the sun shines,' she said, peering through the rain at the orchards. 'What a pity the storm is blowing all the blossom off those trees.' Torn white petals were blowing like confetti past the car, many of them sticking to the windows in the rain. Suddenly the car began to make a strange choking sound, and Alex muttered under his breath. Staring through the windscreen, Deborah said anxiously, 'Alex, the bonnet...'

Thin coils of steam curled up at the sides of the bonnet. Alex groaned. 'That damned radiator! We're running out of water to cool the engine and the car is overheating.'

At that moment she caught a glimpse of a green roof through the curtain of rain. 'Is that the house?'

The steam was growing quickly. Alex slowed the

car to a crawl, grimly watching the bonnet. 'We may just get there before it does too much damage,' he said. 'We'll have to ring the nearest garage and get them to fit a new radiator. I suspected it was badly dented. It must be full of holes. We've been losing water ever since we hit that tree.'

He pulled up a hundred yards from the house. A cloud of steam was rising from the bonnet by then. 'I dare not lift it or the engine will be drowned in rain,' he said irritably. He opened the door and got out. Deborah followed and they began to run towards the house, drenched before they had gone more than a short way. Lightning split the dark sky. She gave an instinctive cry of fright, and Alex looked back at her. 'It can't hurt you,' he said flatly. 'If you can see it, it can be nowhere near you. You're quite safe.'

'I don't like it,' she confessed, putting down her head and running harder towards the house.

She barely got a glimpse of it before they were at the front door. Alex banged loudly on it, pushing Deborah under the slight overhang of the lintel to escape the worst of the rain. There was no answer. He banged with his fist, shouting, 'Mother, it's Alex!'

Silence answered them. She looked at him questioningly. 'What are we going to do?'

Alex tried the door, but it was locked. 'Stay here,' he said grimly, moving round the side of the house. Deborah leaned against the door, her chest heaving after her running, brushing the wet hair out of her eyes. Thunder rolled again and again as if it reverberated around the hills. Through a line of willows she saw the muddy brown waters of the river whirling rapidly, realising that the cottage stood a mere hundred feet from the green banks.

Hearing the front door open, she turned, expecting to see a stranger, but it was not Alex's mother, but

Alex himself. 'I had to break the kitchen window,' he said tersely. 'Get in before you drown.'

She went into the house, finding herself in a narrow vestibule, from which led two doors at right angles. Alex shut the front door and pushed her through one of the others. In astonishment and bewilderment she surveyed a totally empty room. She turned towards him, her eyes wide. 'Alex ...'

'I've seen it,' he said grimly. 'All the furniture has gone. Even the kitchen is practically bare. There's not a sign of anything.'

'Your mother must have moved,' she said faintly. Her eyes stared at him, taking in all the implications of their discovery. She swallowed. 'There's no one here and ...' Her voice trailed away in alarm.

His mouth hard, he said, 'The car's out of action. It's miles to the next village and I don't propose to walk through that storm, anyway. We're stuck here, like it or not.'

She felt like bursting into tears. 'How can we get back to Nice in time to catch our plane?'

He surveyed her unsmilingly. 'We can't,' he said tersely.

Her face went white. She backed away from him, staring at him with bitterly angry eyes. 'You planned it,' she burst out. 'You've brought me here deliberately. You knew very well the house was empty. You've trapped me!'

Alex's face darkened in rage. He advanced towards her too quickly for her to be able to evade him. His hands bit into her shoulders, shaking her violently. 'And I suppose I deliberately ran the car into that tree, did I? And talked you into coming with me? What the hell do you think I am? After last night I'd rather be trapped in a snakepit than cooped up alone with you, you cold-blooded little bitch!' His eyes blazed at her contemptuously. 'You're perfectly safe with me, Deborah. I have no intention of touching you. I can't even stand the sight of you.'

'Or my touch,' she flung, unbearably wounded by what he said, and remembering his reaction when she touched him in the car.

His lips drew back in a snarl. 'Who asked you to touch me? In future keep your hands away from me. We have to stay here until the rain stops, but there's no reason why we should stay in the same room. You can go and see what there is to eat in the kitchen. I expect Mother left a few odd items. I'll go up and look around upstairs. We're best apart, you and I. When we get back to London you can leave the firm and take your three months' pay with you. It'll be worth a few hundred quid to get rid of you.'

'You can keep your money,' she said bitterly. 'I'll be too glad to get away from you to give a damn about it.'

Alex flung her away violently and slammed out of the room. She heard his feet on the uncarpeted stairs, then the silence settled back, bringing with it the unceasing swish of the rain in the sky outside. Lightning crashed again, followed soon by thunder. Deborah sighed deeply, then she began to look for the kitchen.

The cottage was small, she found, built on a slight slope above the river. Two steps led from the empty room in which she stood to the small kitchen beyond. Wall cupboards and an ancient kitchen range were all it contained apart from the sink. She opened the cupboards and was surprised and relieved to find a number of tins, but nothing perishable. There was neither sugar nor tea, neither coffee nor bread. They would be able to eat, anyway, she sighed, and presumably drink water.

The house was chill. She shivered, prowling around the kitchen. They would have to light a fire, but there seemed to be no form of kindling anywhere. Maybe

Alex could find some wood in one of the small outbuildings she could glimpse from the window. She had no coat with her. It was going to get colder.

Alex's voice called her from above, and she went through into the vestibule and went upstairs. He was on the landing. The floor, she was interested to see, was carpeted. Then, through an open door, she saw furniture, and went into the room with an expression of surprise, finding herself in a large bedroom. It contained a bed, stripped bare, and the usual bedroom furniture, comfortable and a little old-fashioned. She looked round at Alex, her heart turning over in alarm again. He looked back at her with a savage smile.

'Providential for the plan you think I'm cherishing, isn't it?' he asked unpleasantly.

She drew a shaky breath. 'All right, Alex, I'll apologise. I didn't really believe you planned it.'

'Didn't you?' His tone was scathing. His eyes ran down her body, stripping her deliberately with their angry gaze. 'Now that you've put the idea into my head it might not be such a bad one. If we're here long, boredom may drive me to amuse myself in your direction.'

'That isn't funny, Alex,' she retorted, stung.

'Isn't it? I think it's very funny,' he said sourly. 'You do realise, I suppose, that Robin is never going to believe you missed that plane by accident? When you don't come back for this precious weekend with his family he'll assume you preferred to spend it in bed with me.'

Deborah's face burned. She turned away and walked out of the room to explore the other rooms. There was a tiny bathroom, she discovered, and one other room, a low-ceilinged room which was stacked with canvases and the other apparatus of painting; an easel, scores of tubes of paints, brushes and many other objects which seemed to litter the place, so that there was very little room to move since the room itself was tiny.

'My mother's studio,' Alex said flatly.

'It's in a terrible mess,' she said, dismayed by such disorder.

He looked at her contemptuously. 'Yes, that's all that would strike you. What a mundane mind you have, Deborah!' The cruel lips twisted. 'Or should I say Miss Portman? Maybe we should revert to our formal relationship again. Since we've been in France we seem to have lapsed into intimacy, and that would never do, would it?'

She forced down a desire to hit him. 'I've found some tins of food,' she said flatly. 'I can make us a supper of sorts if you could light that old range.'

'There should be plenty of wood in the woodshed,' he said, his voice tight. 'I'll see what I can do.'

'We ought to have a fire in one of the rooms downstairs,' she said. 'The house is very cold and we have no coats with us.'

'Where are we going to eat?' he asked sardonically. 'Not in the bedroom, I presume. It might give me the wrong ideas.'

'We'll eat in the room beside the fire you light,' she said, ignoring him. 'I found plates and cutlery in the cupboards.' Her brows creased. 'It's very odd, all the same. Why should your mother clear the whole downstairs like this yet leave the things upstairs?'

'She was probably moving into the village but something stopped them in the middle of it,' he said, shrugging. 'We'll find out tomorrow.'

'I'll start making that meal, then,' she said. 'I think you'd better get that stove started first. If you can't manage it I expect I can always cook on the fire.'

He looked at her in sarcastic mockery. 'So efficient, Miss Portman.'

Lightning tore the sky apart and she gave a shriek of

fear. Alex stared at her, his eyes narrowed. 'Yet you have oddly disarming feminine characteristics,' he said heavily. 'Who would have believed you were so afraid of lightning?' His grey eyes brooded on her. 'What else frightens you, Deborah?'

For a moment their eyes held, then she turned and went downstairs to begin the meal.

CHAPTER SIX

DEBORAH searched the cupboard, trying to decide which of the tins to use. Alex went darting out into the rain, a newspaper he had found carried over his head. She decided to start with one of the tins of soup followed by a tin of ham served with asparagus tips. She was about to open them, sighing over the lack of choice, when Alex came back, carrying a bundle of wood under one arm, a garden trug under the other. He grinned at her, his face triumphant. 'Eggs,' he announced, depositing the trug on the range.

She peered incredulously at the heaped eggs. 'Where on earth ...?'

'My mother's chickens,' he explained cheerfully. 'They have a run up at the end of the garden under some trees. I took a look in their nesting boxes and found these ... some of them were sitting on them, and I suspect no one has been near them for several days. But it will help for supper, won't it?'

'It's marvellous,' she said delightedly. 'How about lobster bisque followed by asparagus omelette?'

His brows rose. 'Good God, I knew you were efficient, Miss Portman, but that sounds like a miracle!'

'Courtesy of your mother's larder,' she grinned. 'The eggs will be much nicer than ham and asparagus, don't you think?'

His eyes were restlessly moving down her body. 'You're soaked to the skin, Deb,' he said thickly. 'You should change out of those wet things.'

She glance down at herself and flushed hotly, realising how her saturated top revealed what lay underneath. 'What am I supposed to change into?' she asked defiantly.

'My mother must have something suitable upstairs,' he said. 'I'll light this range. You go and change, then I'll light a fire in the other room and you can hang your wet clothes in front of it to dry.'

'You should change too,' she pointed out. 'You're as wet as I am.'

'If you think I'm going about in my mother's clothes you can think again,' he said scathingly.

She laughed and went upstairs. His mother was obviously small, she thought in dismay, eyeing the clothes hanging there. They were all much too small for her. She flicked them along their rail and stared at a loose white smock hanging there. It was a little too short, but it was so loosely cut that it would at least cover her. She lifted it down and stripped, then put it on and looked at herself in the mirror uneasily. It only stretched to her thigh just above her knee. However, it covered her, she thought grimly. On the point of leaving she caught sight of a large green box from which dangled a tag clearly marked with Alex's name. The card made it clear that it was a birthday present. She smiled, then, curiosity getting the better of her, lifted the lid and peeped inside. Seeing it was a black quilted silk garment, she took the lid right off and pulled it out. It might do for him to wear while his wet clothes dried, she thought in excitement.

Seeing, with a smile, what it was she carried the box down to the kitchen, her wet clothes dangling over her arm. She found Alex kneeling in front of the empty grate in the bare sitting-room. He looked at her over his shoulder, then his eyes narrowed. 'Very fetching,' he said roughly.

Ignoring the remark, Deborah held out the box. 'Guess what I found upstairs in the wardrobe.'

He looked at it frowning. 'It must be my birthday present. I can't open it now, she'd never forgive me. My birthday isn't for a week.'

'I peeped inside,' she admitted. 'I think you should open it. It's heaven-sent.'

Reluctantly Alex took the box. Opening it, he lifted out the black garment and a faint grin crossed his face. 'I see what you mean.' He put it back into his mother's box, pushed it on to the floor and turned back to the work he was engaged upon. 'I've lit the range. You get on with the supper. I'm ravenous. Leave your clothes and I'll hang them out.'

'What on?' she asked anxiously. 'It's dangerous to leave wet clothes too near a fire.'

'There's an old brass fireguard in the woodshed,' he said. 'I'm going to get it in a minute. Deb, get on with the food.'

'You should change,' she protested.

'And get soaked every time I go outside?' he asked patiently. 'I've got a number of things to do before I change into dry things.'

She went through into the kitchen and began to inspect the range. It looked more complicated than it was, and she began to work out how it operated after a while. Alex had lit a good fire and the hobs were warming up nicely. She assembled all the things she needed and set to work.

Alex walked outside into the pouring rain a few moments later. He returned with a brass fireguard, sniffing at the delicious odour of the food. 'You're getting on well,' he commented. 'How's the range behaving?'

'Fine,' she said. 'But could you bring in some more wood later? It burns very quickly.'

'I'll bring in stacks of wood before I change,' he nodded. 'I don't fancy having to run outside in the rain in the dark. I've found some paraffin lamps out there, thank God, and enough paraffin, too.'

Deborah stared. 'Why do you want paraffin?'

He looked at her, sighing. 'Deb, it's clear you've never lived in the country. In a storm the electricity sometimes goes and then we'll need paraffin lamps.'

She groaned. 'This is getting too complicated!' Then she stared at him. 'Alex, the phone ... why didn't I think of that? You can ring and get someone to collect us.'

His face was patient. 'I thought of that the first moment we arrived, but the phone is dead. Either Mother had it cut off or ...' He shrugged. 'In this storm the line may be dead.'

She sighed. 'Oh, well ...'

He carried the fireguard through the door and she went on with her cooking. Alex went back and forth after that, carting wood into the house, stacking it in a corner of the firelit room. The darkness was now falling faster. Deborah could not see the garden at all. Finally Alex washed his hands at the sink, shrugged, and said, 'I'm finished now. Have I got time to change before we eat? I'm frozen!'

'Of course,' she said anxiously. 'I hope you haven't caught a chill.'

'I'll take off my things beside the fire,' he said. 'I won't be a moment.'

She had finished cooking. The lobster bisque steamed fragrantly in two bowls. The omelettes were ready, kept warm between two plates above a saucepan of hot water. Giving him time to change, she carried the soup into the room, tapping on the door before she entered. 'Come in, Deb,' he said curtly. He was draping his wet clothes across the fireguard, she found, alongside her own. Steam rose from them. The air in the room was so cold she shivered. Alex gave her a grim look.

'We'll eat in the kitchen,' he said. 'It'll be warmer near the stove. The only chairs we have are my mother's studio chairs. They're rickety and filthy, but at least we can sit down.'

Sighing, Deborah returned to the kitchen. A moment later Alex carried down the two chairs. Cane-bottomed, weak-legged, they looked very unsafe to her, but obediently she sat down on one. Alex sat, too, and they drank their soup. The range was giving the room a new warmth, although cold air and rain blew in through the window Alex had broken to make his entry. He looked it over irritably, then found the newspaper he had used to cover his head and stuffed it into the jagged hole. The room was appreciably warmer after that. They ate their omelettes in a silence which was not unpleasant. The sound of the storm outside made the lamplit kitchen more cosy, and Deborah's legs grew warmer as she held her toes towards the iron range.

The range gave out a faintly smoky atmosphere which made her feel gradually sleepy. She leaned forward, warming her hands at it.

'How long do you think my clothes will take to dry?' she asked Alex absently.

'The sooner the better,' he said tightly.

She looked round at him in surprise. His eyes were on the long bare expanse of her slender thighs, exposed by the brevity of the white smock. Through her lashes she surveyed him. His mother's birthday present had been a quilted dressing-gown. It covered no more of him than her smock did of her, but the black silk gave him a magnificence which made her heart quicken.

'I suppose your mother paints in this?' she asked him to divert his attention.

'Yes,' he said vaguely. His eyes lifted to her face. 'It looks better on you,' he said directly.

She smiled, flushing. 'Thank you.'

'Don't be coy, Deb,' he said tightly. 'You know you're lovely.'

'It's pleasant to be told I am,' she said softly.

Alex stood up. 'We'd better wash up,' he said harshly.

She followed and they tidied the room together, working in harmony, hardly saying a word. Her mind was preoccupied with the problem of where they were to sleep. There was only one bedroom and she had no intention of sharing it with Alex. Could one of them use his mother's studio? The thought of clearing that clutter was too wearying at this hour. There was only the downstairs room.

Licking her lips nervously, she said, 'I think I'll sleep by the fire downstairs. It'll be cosy down there.'

He looked at her savagely. 'I wondered how long it would take that busy little brain of yours to work out that we would have a problem there,' he said. 'You can sleep in the bedroom. I'll sleep by the fire.'

'Let's toss for it,' she said brightly.

His arm gripped her suddenly, his hand biting into her waist. Inches away from her face he snarled, 'Don't argue with me. You'll sleep upstairs, I'll sleep down here. You can get to bed now.'

She dared not protest in the face of that stony expression. 'Well, thank you,' she stammered. 'Goodnight, Alex.' She paused. 'You'll need bedclothes—it'll get cold during the night. I'll take a look upstairs.'

She searched around and found an ottoman which held spares; sheets, blankets, duvets, pillows. Alex was in the room beside the fire when she found him. The paraffin lamp smoked slightly on the mantel. His dark head was casting a shadow on the wall behind him as he inspected the row of damp clothes hanging on the guard. She saw his hands pick up her shirt, holding it, staring down at it.

She moved and he turned, putting it down. They

stared at each other across the room. 'I found some bedclothes,' she said huskily. Alex came towards her, throwing an enormous shadow across the ceiling and wall. It seemed to tower over her, black and commanding. He took the bundle she offered him and tossed it to the floor.

'Go to bed, Deb,' he said thickly.

She lingered, unwilling to leave him. 'Are you sure you'll be comfortable down here? The floor must be hard.'

'Are you offering to let me share your bed, Deb?' he asked her unpleasantly.

She flushed, shaking her head. 'I thought we might rig up something more comfortable ...'

'I'll survive,' he said. 'Oh, for God's sake, get out of here!'

She left him, her body trembling. She slid into the bed she had made up some time later and turned down the paraffin lamp until it died. In the darkness she could hear the rain continuing to lash against the windows. The thunder and lightning rumbled occasionally, but it seemed further away. By morning it should be possible for them to walk to the next village, she thought, snuggling under the blankets. The bed was deeply comfortable. Her lids closed. Poor Alex! He would have an uncomfortable night on the hard floor.

Sleep crept over her as she thought about him, and somehow he accompanied her into her dreams, dominating them as he had dominated the room downstairs with his giant black shadow, looming over her in close pursuit. She awoke with a start, at first unable to remember where she was, then, looking round the unfamiliar darkness of the room, remembering and wondering what time it was now.

She fumbled for her watch and looked at it, unwilling to light the paraffin lamp again. Lightning still zipped down the sky outside. It had moved even further away, thought Deborah. She slid out of the bed and went to the window to look out, hoping she might see the time by the next flash. The flash came a few moments later. Her eyes on her watch, she saw with surprise that it was four o'clock. She must have slept for longer than she had thought. It had been ten when she went to bed.

Thunder rolled around the sky. The storm had lasted for hours, she thought. She leaned on the narrow sill staring into the darkness. Rain sluiced down ceaselessly. Was Alex asleep? she wondered. Restlessly, she was about to move away when the lightning flared again and by its brief light she saw water flooding across the garden.

She frowned. Water? Her body tensed and she turned to run across the room and down the stairs. Water was already washing under the door sill. Splashing through it, she went into the room Alex was using. He had rolled himself up beside the fire, his back towards her. She ran to him, shaking his shoulder. 'Alex ... wake up!'

He had built up the fire and it smouldered redly, giving the room a faint glow. By the light of that warmth Alex's still sleepy eyes travelled up her body. His hand reached out to stroke her bare calf. 'Deb,' he said in a muffled voice.

'Wake up,' she said urgently. 'The river is flooding. It's coming into the house!'

Alex seemed to snap into awareness instantly. He uncoiled and stood beside her, still wearing his dressing-gown. Striding across the room, he opened the door and water ebbed softly into the room. He swore beneath his breath. 'God, that explains everything!'

'What?' she asked, bewildered.

'The empty rooms,' he said impatiently. 'Mother has shifted all her pictures and ornaments, her furniture,

DUEL OF DESIRE

and gone to the village. They're safely on high ground there. She knew the water wouldn't reach the upstairs rooms. Don't you see? That was what she was babbling about on the phone, but the line was so bad I couldn't get her drift.'

'What shall we do?' she asked him anxiously.

He stared at the floor, a frown on his face. 'There's a fireplace in Mother's bedroom. We'll take all the wood up there. We'll have to carry as much food as we can, too. God knows how high the river may rise. We may be marooned up there for a day or so.'

'We won't be able to cook,' she said, biting her lip. 'There's nowhere to cook up there.'

'The stove will be out of action down here,' he said impatiently. 'But there's a one-ring paraffin stove in the studio, or at least there used to be. We'll have to make the best of it.'

'I thought it was bad enough,' she said despairingly, 'but it's getting worse.'

'I'm sorry, Deb,' Alex said flatly. 'But you were the one who insisted on coming.'

The water was growing deeper as they talked. Alex picked up a load of wood and moved towards the stairs. Deborah followed him, a bundle under her own arm. They worked as quickly as they could, shifting the wood. Their clothes were dry now, so she took them upstairs, and then went back to help shift the food and crockery from the kitchen. It was half an hour before they had moved everything, and by then the water was obviously much deeper. Alex stood on the bottom stair, calculating the rise. 'I don't think it will get much higher,' he said.

'You're just trying to comfort me,' she accused, her lower lip trembling.

He looked at her, sighing. 'You're in no danger from drowning,' he promised.

They heard a long hiss from the other room as the water reached the fire, and Deborah shivered. 'Water is terrifying like this,' he said.

He turned. 'Come upstairs,' he said gently. 'You're tired. You must get some more sleep.'

In the bedroom she moved towards the bed, then halted, flushing. 'What about you? I mean ...'

'I'll sleep on the floor,' he said abruptly. 'I'll use the studio.'

'It's like an ice box in there,' she protested. She pulled back her covers and slid into the bed. 'Get in,' she said tightly.

Alex stared at her across the room, his face grim. 'You know I can't sleep with you, Deb. Robin would never believe it was innocent.'

'Robin isn't here,' she said irritably. 'Your feet are wet and you're cold. I can't let you die of pneumonia. Put out the lamp and get into bed.' She turned over on to her side and shifted to the far side of the bed. After a long pause the light went out. Heart thudding, she felt Alex slip into the bed. The covers were pulled up further and a pillow shifted. She felt it slide between them.

'I haven't got a sword to put between us,' he said sardonically. 'That will have to do.'

Deborah didn't answer, fighting bitter disappointment. She knew, hating herself, that she had hoped to feel the hard warmth of his body against her back. Silence lay between them. Suddenly she shifted, wriggling to get comfortable. The bed was too narrow for both of them, and the pillow made it worse. Her foot brushed Alex's foot and she was shocked by the clamminess of his skin.

She sat up, peering at him through the darkness. All she could see of his face was a pale oval. She could make out no features. 'Your feet are frozen,' she said, almost accusingly. 'And they're trembling. I'm sure you've caught a chill.'

'I'm fine,' he said tersely. 'Go to sleep, for God's sake.'

She hesitated for a few seconds, trying to decide what to do, then taking a deep breath pulled the pillow out from between them. Leaning over, she touched his forehead. It seemed hot to her, and he moved restlessly as her fingers moved across it. 'I'm sure you've got a temperature,' she said anxiously. 'I told you not to go around for so long in those wet clothes.'

'I'm perfectly all right,' he snapped on a flare of irritation. 'Stop fussing over me!'

'You've got to keep warm,' she said nervously.

His breathing suddenly quickened. 'What do you suggest?' he asked in an unsteady voice.

Deborah lay down again, turning her back on him. 'We'll have to sleep close together,' she said, trying to sound calmly efficient. 'There's no other way.'

For a moment he lay still, then his body rolled near her, and she felt him curve himself around her back, his hands moving round her to pull her back against him. She could sense the warmth of his breathing between her shoulder-blades. 'Like this, you mean?' he asked softly, mockery in his voice now.

She tried to relax, but it was impossible while he held her so intimately. Suddenly he whispered, 'Do you really expect me to sleep, Deb?'

'Why not?' she asked in a voice she hoped sounded casual. 'We're both suffering from exhaustion.'

He laughed. 'Curiouser and curiouser, Miss Portman. You're beginning to sound almost human.' The teasing in his voice was interrupted when he sneezed violently.

'I knew you'd caught a chill,' she said anxiously.

'Oh, God,' he swore irritably, 'that's all I need!'

For a while they lay in silence. She breathed regularly, hoping sleep would come. The coldness was seeping away as she felt the warmth of Alex's body close to her back. Discreetly she moved her foot in an effort to find out if his feet were warmer now. They certainly felt less cold, and he sighed as she touched him. She yawned, her body relaxing. Drowsiness crept over her. The rain still poured down outside, drumming against the roof and windows, but the sound of the storm had ceased, and she began to find the noise of the rain hypnotic. Alex seemed to be asleep. His hands were clasped against her midriff, their pressure disturbing. She softly moved them up a little, then she lay thinking about the flood waters. Surely they were safe from them up here? The water would not rise as high as the upper storey. Without noticing it she drifted into unconsciousness which sank over her like the dark waters of the flood.

Birdsong awoke her. She lay without moving, dazedly aware that something was unusual, then she became alert, realising at a rush that she lay curled against Alex's chest, her face pillowed on his bare shoulder, the comforting rise and fall beneath her the movements of his sleeping body. During the night she must have turned over.

She remembered everything immediately. Not daring to move, she listened to the sound of his breathing. It seemed shallow to her. She frowned. Was his chill worse, after all? Tentatively moving her head, she turned so that she could look up at him. Under her warm cheek his skin felt as though his temperature was normal. Looking up at him through her lashes she saw him at an odd angle, the hard chin dark with stubble, his lids closed, a fringe of dark lashes along his cheekbones. She lifted one hand and delicately touched his chin. Under her fingers the dark hairs prickled pleasantly.

Alex's chin tilted. The silvery eyes opened and looked down into her face.

For a moment they merely looked at each other. Her body still lay against him, warmly relaxed. Her mouth quivered into a smile.

'Did you sleep well?'

'Yes,' he said, sounding surprised. His hand moved to push back a strand of tousled hair from her face. 'So this is what you look like first thing in the morning!'

'A mess,' she interpreted, wrinkling her nose.

'Don't fish for compliments,' he teased, his hand returning to tighten around her body.

She felt a twinge of warning. 'I'll get up and boil some of those eggs for our breakfast,' she told him.

'Not yet,' he said, his voice deepening. Before she could move he rolled her on to her back and leaned over her, looking down at her.

'Don't spoil it, Alex,' she said angrily. 'This situation is difficult enough without making things worse.'

'I'm not Robin,' he said cuttingly. 'You're not turning me into a tame little man about the house, Deb. Last night you surprised and impressed me by suggesting we sleep together to keep warm. I thought you showed unexpected humanity. But later I realised how insulting the suggestion was ... as soon as you thought I had a chill you started treating me like a harmless child, fussing over me soothingly. I don't intend to be treated that way by you or any woman.'

She looked at him scornfully. 'Your male ego hurt, Alex? You prefer to play the big bad wolf, is that it? You value that machismo image of yours, don't you? You would have preferred it if I'd locked myself into this room, shivering in terror, forcing you to sleep in an icy room all night. It fits in better with the way you see yourself. Sorry I didn't play the game by your rules, but I couldn't let you catch pneumonia even to pander to your ego.'

'Damn you!' he ground furiously, his face red. 'You're twisting everything to suit yourself. That isn't how I see myself.'

'Isn't it? You've played the part so long you no longer even know it is a part,' she said. Her eyes blazed blue fire at him. 'Alex St James has to be irresistible, striking fear and fascination into every woman he meets, forcing them to admit they can't resist him, then moving on with a shrug to the next target. It makes lovely reading in the popular papers, Alex, but there's nothing much behind the alluring image, is there? All tinsel and glitter on top, but underneath there's just a vacuum...'

His face tightened until the bones beneath the skin stood out. His eyes pierced her face bitterly. 'You bitch,' he said under his breath. 'You acid-tongued little bitch ...' His hands wrenched at her trailing hair, tilting her face upward towards him, and his mouth closed savagely over hers, forcing her lips back on to her teeth in a brief but deliberately cruel kiss. When it was over she lay, shivering, her tongue probing the torn flesh of her inner lip, staring at him with hatred.

'You swine,' she said huskily. 'That's your only answer, to use force if your famous charm fails, isn't it? You sicken me! I'd rather swim to the next village than spend another night here alone with you.'

Alex rolled away and slid out of the bed. 'Swim, then,' he said harshly. 'I hope you drown. I'm going to the bathroom. When I come back I shall get dressed. If you don't want to watch me you'd better get out of bed now and get dressed and out of here.' Stalking across the room, he slammed the door behind him.

Deborah winced as the sound rang in her ears. Her angry attack on him had been fuelled more by fear than anger. The erotic pressure of his body against her had made her only too aware of the weakness of her defences against him. Had he chosen to exert the charm of which she had been so scathing she could never have resisted him. Even while he snapped at her she had been consumed with a need to soothe him into smiling at her, but she had fought it down with difficulty, forcing herself to launch a counter-attack in order to rebuild her shattered defences.

Hurriedly she dressed, her mouth still aching from the savagery of his assault on her. She had not expected his reaction to be so violent. He had always been sharply barbed in his attitude to her, but in the past few days he had grown increasingly savage. Had he felt afraid that some truth lay behind her accusations? Alex was too intelligent not to know that the building of a public image always carried with it the danger that one might come to believe in it oneself. It was a danger which threatened some of their artistes, one which they had often been forced to deal with when the image took over the human being and brought disaster with it.

Her cotton top seemed to have shrunk. She pulled it down, trying to get it to meet her jeans, but a pale line of midriff still showed. While she was tugging at it Alex returned. Their eyes met across the room warily. He had a masked expression, the rage absent from his face.

'I'm sorry,' he said stiffly. 'I behaved badly.'

Deborah sighed, relaxing, having half expected further trouble. 'I suppose we're both under a strain,' she said quietly. 'We're in a difficult situation and we must try to adjust to it.'

He nodded grimly. 'You have a genius for understatement. The situation may be "difficult" to you, but I find it intolerable.'

'I'm sorry,' she said helplessly.

Alex sneezed and swore under his breath.

She was tempted to smile, touched by his small-boy irritation with the cold. 'You'd better light the fire,' she said softly. 'You mustn't neglect that cold.'

He looked at her hard. 'Don't fuss over me, Deb. I've got to get dressed.' He reached over to the chair on which she had placed the pile of his clothes and pulled his jeans up. His hand went to the belt of his dressing-gown and Deborah hurriedly went out of the room.

Curiously she peered down the stairs. The sunlight reflected on water lapping along the third stair from the bottom. How long would it be before the water went down? she wondered, turning into the bathroom.

Ten minutes later, feeling refreshed after a leisurely wash, she began to hunt among the piled objects in the small studio looking for the portable stove Alex thought might be among them. She found it after a while, battered and dusty, among a pile of books. Judith would get on with Alex's mother, she thought, her mouth denting humorously. They both had no sense of order. Her eyes roved over the room. If she had time she would restore it to some sort of tidiness. Curiously, she flicked over a stack of canvases against one wall. Most of them were paintings of flowers or fruit, but one of them made her pause, her heart thudding.

She pulled it out and stood it against the wall, staring at it with fascination.

A portrait of Alex, it showed his head and shoulders against a stormy sky, the colour of which was almost identical to the colour of those silvery eyes. His mother had exactly caught a characteristic expression. Hard, forceful yet strangely vulnerable, the features had been drawn with understanding and love, even a kind of pity which Deborah felt reflected the way she herself felt towards him.

'Deb, the fire's lit. Where are my eggs?' His voice made her jump guiltily, catching her staring at his picture with her feelings in her eyes.

She turned, making her mouth smile formally. 'Just coming!'

Alex saw what she had been looking at, and came slowly into the room, staring at it too.

'I've never seen that before,' he said in surprise. He lifted it and stood it perched on top of the stack of others, inspecting it with a frown. 'Mother's never had the knack of portraits,' he said, dismissively.

Deborah said nothing, wondering if he resented that betraying look about the eyes and mouth which had struck her so much in the picture.

He glanced at her, his eyes defensive. 'Not very good, is it?'

'It's brilliant,' she said gently.

His cheeks flushed and he turned away. 'Even if you aren't hungry, I am,' he said. 'After breakfast we'll see what damage the floods have done. I'll have to take a look at the poor damned chickens. I left their run open so that they could take cover if the water rose ...' His voice broke off and they stared at each other.

'You knew,' she said, understanding in a flash.

Alex hesitated, then gave a grimace. 'It occurred to me last night when I saw how high the river was, but I saw no point in frightening the life out of you, and there was a possibility the rain might stop before the water came over the banks.'

She was not sure whether to believe him or not. He might have brought her here deliberately, hoping they would be marooned alone, but surely if he had planned this he would not have been so hostile to her? Had he planned a seduction he would have had a perfect opportunity last night, yet he had been irritable rather than charming, and nothing in his behaviour had indicated that he was other than furious with the situation in which they were trapped. Had he brought her here before their bitter quarrel after dinner at Ricky's villa she might have suspected his motives, but he had been too genuinely angry with her, too savage and hostile, for her to believe he had meant this to happen.

He watched the struggle in her eyes, and said unpleasantly, 'I assure you, you're the last woman in the world I would have wanted to be stuck here with, Miss Portman.' His mouth twisted cynically. 'Any other woman might have made the experience pleasurable, but spending so long cooped up with you is purgatory. If I'd wanted to be marooned here with a woman I'd have picked someone who would know how to help the time pass amusingly.'

As she passed him she asked sarcastically, 'Someone like Sammy Starr, for instance? She doesn't seem to mind if you use her as a toy for your idle moments. I would have thought a girl with her looks and talent had more self-respect.'

Alex followed her into the bedroom. 'Sammy would find all this great fun,' he said deliberately. 'She's very adaptable.'

'The word describes her perfectly,' she said. 'I would hate to hear it used about me.'

'You never will,' he assured her. 'You're as adaptable as granite.'

'Where's the paraffin?' she asked, prickling with irritation at this description of herself. 'Can you get this stove working?'

'Give it here,' he said, taking it from her hand. As he moved the silver medallion Sammy had given him swung into view, and she caught it, staring at it with dislike.

Alex looked down at her, eyes narrowing, and her mouth curled. 'She should have had it inscribed,' she said bitingly. 'For services rendered.'

His eyes glinted. 'You've never liked Sammy, have you? With any other woman I'd suspect jealousy.'

Her eyes darkened, but she kept them lowered. 'I admire her as a singer. She's a great entertainer.' Her lashes flickered up in bitter sarcasm. 'In every sense of the word.'

He looked amused. 'Is it possible you're being feline, Miss Portman? That cool manner is slipping. But you're right, Sammy is very entertaining—in every sense of the word.'

Her hand tightened on the medallion. Without stopping to consider the consequences she jerked on it and the chain snapped. She flung it across the room, her face bitter.

Alex stiffened, watching her, and she heard him draw a sharp breath. 'Well, well,' he said huskily.

Deborah swallowed, horrified by what she had done. 'I'm sorry,' she said quickly, 'I didn't mean to do that.' She turned away, fumblingly picking up some eggs. 'Could you do the stove right away? I'll get some water in a saucepan. Will the water in the bathroom be safe to use?'

She was horribly afraid that he would pursue the matter, but for some reason he calmly said, 'Yes, I think so, as you'll boil it.'

She walked into the bathroom and leaned her hot face against the wall. For a moment she had lost her self-control, jealous of that constant reminder of Sammy Starr, and she bitterly wished she had kept her head. It was far too easy for her to forget that she had, at all costs, to stop Alex from discovering she loved him. Beneath his angry hostility that physical awareness still prickled between them, making it hard for her to keep him at a distance. This morning, lying warmly in his arms, she had wanted desperately to surrender to him. It would have been so fatally easy, so exquisitely satisfactory. She had deliberately picked a quarrel with him to stop herself from doing what she wanted to do, and then she had spoiled it by a stupid gesture of jealous anger. He was too shrewd, too experienced, to fail to put two and two together. Her only hope was that he thought cynically that although she secretly wanted to go to bed with him she refused to admit the fact, either to him or herself, and her jealousy of Sammy was purely based on envy because Sammy did not suffer from the same iron will power. Even a belief that she was envious of Sammy's easy attitude to sex was preferable to the idea that Alex might begin to suspect she was actually in love with him. If he knew she loved him she would suffer agonies of humiliation.

CHAPTER SEVEN

WHEN they had eaten their boiled eggs and drunk a bottle of Vichy water which Alex had produced from a corner of his mother's studio, they stared out of the window at the astonishing blue of the sky. The weather had veered round. All traces of the storm had gone except for the glinting water which still stood almost knee deep in the garden and across the road. The spring sun shone down over the orchards, filtering through the blossom-laden branches. Some of the branches had lost their blossom. White petals, speckled brown by rain and wind, floated on top of the flood, like drifting snow. Against the blue of the sky the blossom had a fresh bridal sweetness which caught at the heart. Deborah remembered the fragility of the trees last night, flung helplessly to and fro by the lashing wind. This morning they stood in calm serenity with the sky drifting overhead in halcyon gentleness, as if it had never darkened into storm and passion.

'How long do you think it will be before the water recedes?' she asked Alex.

'I've no idea,' he shrugged. 'Perhaps we should send out a dove.'

She laughed. 'Could we wade to the village?'

'I don't fancy the idea,' he said. 'We've no wellingtons and I've no wish to swim.' He sneezed violently, his forehead flushed.

'That cold is getting worse,' she said, looking at him with worried blue eyes. 'I think you should go back to bed.'

'Well, I'm not going,' he snapped. 'Although I

wouldn't refuse a whisky and hot lemon.'

Taking him seriously, she said, 'There's no whisky,' her brow creased.

He grinned, his eyes teasing her. 'No lemons, either. So I'll just have to go without. I'm good at that.' His tone brought a sudden wary look into her blue eyes.

She turned away from the window. 'Well, I think I'll tidy up your mother's studio. She can't enjoy working in that mess.'

'Don't make it too tidy, Deb,' he said quickly. 'Mother might resent it. She works best in a clutter.'

'Like Judith,' she said indulgently.

He raised an eyebrow. 'Oh?'

'Judith is chronically untidy,' she said affectionately. 'She can't help it. She sheds objects like a dog shedding hairs. I have to follow her around clearing up after her.'

'I bet she enjoys that,' he said satirically.

She said defensively, 'She and I get on very well. We dovetail. Judith has five thumbs on every hand, so I do all the housework and the cooking, but she's such a super friend that we rarely quarrel about anything. She's funny and clever and entertaining ...' Her words halted as the word reminded her of what had happened earlier, and she felt her face colour.

'Entertaining,' Alex repeated sardonically. 'Obviously I must get to know her better.'

'You know very well what I mean,' she said angrily.

'I never know what you mean, Deb,' he said flatly.

She turned away. 'I'll get on with the studio.'

'Why don't we just sit by the fire and talk?' he asked. 'There's no need for you to rush about doing domestic work. If my mother wanted her studio to look like a show place she'd get someone in to do it, but I tell you she likes clutter.'

'I'm not used to sitting around doing nothing,' she protested, appalled at the prospect. 'There are no books to read, no radio ... nothing.'

Alex's jaw tightened. 'We can talk,' he said, watching her. 'Why are you afraid to talk to me, Deb?'

'Stop thinking of yourself as the irresistible object,' she snapped. 'I'm not afraid to talk to you.'

He pulled the bedroom chair near the fire. 'Sit down, then,' he invited.

'You sit there,' she said. 'I'll sit on a pillow.' She took one from the bed and sat on it, her arms linked around her raised knees, staring at the flickering fire. After a moment Alex sat down in the chair, crossing his legs, his eyes fixed on her profile. Sunlight haloed her head, giving her a glittering aureole. Her lids drooped, her face thoughtful.

'Tell me about your childhood,' he said quietly.

She sighed. 'Nothing to tell. I never knew my parents. Until I was old enough to go to a boarding school I lived with my uncle and a nurse. I barely remember the years before I went to school, except that they were dull. Nothing ever happened. Just little things ... like when it snowed very heavily one winter and I made a giant snowball and rolled it down the hill near our house. It started to go slowly, but it got faster and faster until I fell over and it rolled out of sight. I ran away because I was frightened. I remember a few things like that. Otherwise those years are blank.' She looked at him defensively, feeling an odd reluctance to talk to him about herself. 'How about you? What do you remember of your childhood?'

His silvery eyes were fixed on her face thoughtfully as she turned, but he said after a pause, 'Too many things, I'm afraid. We lived in London and my first memory is of picking willowherb on a bomb site. I must have been about three. I fell over and cut my cheekbone, and there was such a bad gash that Mother took me to a hospital to have some stitches put in it.

She held my hand while they did it and I remember screaming because it hurt. They gave me an injection to prevent tetanus, I suppose.' His hand flicked at his right cheek. 'I still have a scar there.'

Deborah stared, seeing nothing. 'It must be invisible, then. I've never noticed one.'

'Here,' he said, his fingers feeling along his cheekbone. 'Do you see it? I can feel it.' He bent down until their faces were level, his eyes expressionless. Taking her right hand, he ran it over his cheekbone. She felt the tiny sickle-shaped scar after a moment, but she was chiefly aware of the pleasure the tiny contact gave her. Her fingertips ached to go on exploring the hard bones of his face, to trace and discover every atom of his features.

'Feel it?' he asked, watching her face.

'Yes,' she said huskily, trembling with the effort of appearing unmoved.

'You have very capable fingers,' he commented, still holding her hand against his face. 'Cool and clever fingers. What else do you do besides cook and do housework? With hands like these you ought to be good at art.'

Deborah moistened her lips. 'I was good at it at school,' she said nervously, wishing he would release her hand, yet not daring to make a point of it in case she precipitated something worse.

'Do you paint?' As if absently Alex moved her hand downward along his cheekbones, rubbing her palm against his skin, sending prickles of awareness along her nervous system. He had been unable to shave, of course, and the stubble on his face was rough against her.

'Not now,' she said. 'Shall I make the fire up? It seems to be in need of some more wood.' The excuse to have both hands free sounded perfectly natural, she thought.

He glanced at the fire, without releasing her hand.

'It's fine,' he said softly, sounding satirical. 'What about hobbies? Do you do embroidery, make clothes?'

'I went to pottery classes for a year,' she said. 'I enjoyed it and I made some pretty things for the flat, but if I'd wanted to go any further with it I would have had to spend more than one evening a week at it, and I couldn't spare the time.'

'What do you do with your spare time, anyway?' he asked.

'Robin and I go to the theatre,' she said. 'Among other things.'

His eyes chilled. 'Ah, yes, Robin,' he said, as if he had forgotten him. Deliberately he handed her back her hand as if it were an unwanted parcel. 'So you go to the theatre? What does Robin's taste run to? Bawdy comedies or musicals?'

Deborah flushed indignantly. 'No,' she objected. She clasped her hands around her knees again. 'His taste is pretty catholic. We see most of the successful plays.'

'For successful read fashionable,' he retorted. 'Nothing indigestible. Avant-garde if it gets good reviews, and the occasional foreign film which everyone goes to see.'

'Don't snipe at Robin,' she said tautly. 'You don't really know him.'

'I know he's conventional, small-minded, ambitious, lacks any sort of originality or spark.' His tone was biting. 'He'll make a splendid husband for you, Deb. If he's unfaithful to you he'll do it so discreetly you'll never know, and he'll never make you lose your head, and that's important, isn't it? Those feet of yours have to be firmly set on the ground in case you lose your balance. You haven't got the nerve to venture out of the safe harbour Robin offers you and try the open sea. You might get shipwrecked, and that would never do.' The silvery eyes probed her flushed, averted face. She stared into the fire, her eyes angry.

'You're trying to talk about a subject we both know is taboo,' she said fiercely. 'If we're going to talk, let's talk about something safe.'

'Safe!' The word was bitten through taut lips. 'You've got nothing of the gambler in you, have you, Deb? You take no risks, offer no hostages to fortune. What a dull life you're going to have!'

'If you're talking about yourself,' she retorted savagely, suddenly so angry she could barely speak, 'what you fail to see is that I know you well enough to realise that I wouldn't be taking a risk in having an affair with you. I would be gambling on a certainty—the certainty that you aren't capable of making it worth while.'

Alex leant forward and turned her face towards him, glaring at her, the red glare of the fire reflected in his eyes. 'What the hell is that supposed to mean?'

She met his eyes head-on, her face icy. 'What woman wants to be one among a crowd? Do you think the pleasure of going to bed with you is so fantastic that I'd prefer that to a lifetime's happiness with a man who loves me?'

His lip curled. 'If Robin loves you it's because he has the same timid attitude to life as you have. He wants a rabbit hutch of a house and a shiny car and two point five children, or whatever the national average happens to be at the time. Robin wants to conform. You're one of the status symbols he's acquiring in order to be just like all the others.' His fingers tightened on her chin, biting into the soft flesh of her upper throat. 'He's not a demanding lover, is he, Deb? He doesn't make your head reel. If he's been taking you out for months without trying to get you into bed he's barely human.'

'He respects me,' she said, knowing how lame the excuse sounded, even to her own ears, and inwardly feeling almost hysterical when she vigorously defended a man she no longer intended to marry.

'Respects you!' His voice snorted derisively. 'Good God, woman, is respect what you want from a man?' The grey eyes darkened. 'Only a woman with ice water in her veins could want that, and even your cold nature needs more than respect.'

She stiffened. 'What makes you think I'm cold with Robin?' she asked in deliberate provocation, resenting his remark.

Alex's eyes flashed. 'Yes, what makes me think it?' he asked, half to himself. A strange look passed over his face. 'But you've never let him touch you the way I have, have you, Deb?' The question seemed to be forced out of him, half in anger, half in disbelief.

'You don't expect me to describe what Robin does when he makes love to me, do you?' she asked tartly.

A hard red stain grew on his cheekbones. 'What are you trying to do to me, Deb?' he demanded thickly. Both hands framed her face, his thumbs pressing into her throat until it ached. He looked at her with bitter hostility. 'I can't even stand the thought of you in his arms,' he muttered with a savage intonation. 'I have to know. Unlike Robin, I've got a vivid imagination, and the way you respond to me tells me you either want me as much as I want you, or ...' His voice broke off, thickening with anger.

She looked down, her lashes glinting in the firelight. 'Or I'm less inexperienced than you thought?' she suggested sweetly. 'Maybe you shouldn't dismiss Robin so cavalierly after all, Alex.'

He swore violently. 'Under that groomed exterior you're a sharp-clawed little cat, aren't you, Deb?' His thumbs forced themselves into the soft flesh of her throat and she gave a little cry of pain.

'You're hurting!'

'Good,' he said harshly. 'I can force you to accept some experiences, can't I, Deb? If not passion, then pain.'

'Pain would be preferable,' she said sweetly.

He snarled in rage. 'You bitch!' His face swooped down to her, glittering with temper, pushing her head back, those cruel thumbs controlling her, refusing to allow her to escape.

Her own anger at the barbed exchanges made her reckless. She met his punitive lips fiercely. For a second they clashed in silent antagonism, then Alex slid out of his chair and knelt in front of her, his hands loosening from their grip on her throat. Still kissing, they swayed like trees in a stormy wind. Tides of unmanageable feeling beat through her. Alex's hands were moving down her back, clenching on the thin material of her top, pulling her closer. 'You're driving me crazy,' he muttered, reluctantly freeing her mouth. 'You asked for that!'

Deborah was trembling, trying to pull herself together. Running a hand over her swollen mouth, she said shakily, 'I can't think how you got your reputation for making love, Alex. You play very roughly.'

'Only when I'm driven to it,' he retorted.

They stared at each other. He seemed as unable as she was to end the tension between them. Dry tension ached along her face. Her limbs shook with it.

'I think it would be wiser if I tidied the studio,' she said flatly. The ache in the centre of her body was too powerful to bear. She had to get away from him.

He resumed his chair, bending forward to add wood to the fire. The flush on his face might be caused by heat, she thought, but it would not explain the shake she could see in his fingers as he dusted his hands.

She got up and left the room without another word. In the studio she began to work feverishly, moving about in a methodical fashion which disguised the turmoil in which her feelings moved. Whenever she was upset or worried she relieved her tension by work. Restoring order to chaos helped her to ease her feelings. She needed to keep busy at this moment. It stopped her from losing her self-control even further than she had done.

Moving about, sorting through the strange objects she found, she could not stop thinking about Alex's behaviour. It would be mere wishful thinking to let herself believe he cared more about her than a pure desire to go to bed with her, she told herself. His anger and emotion were both based on the frustration he was suffering. She had denied him something he had decided he wanted, and the spoilt little boy still hidden under the gloss of the sophisticated man had burst into enraged rebellion. Their isolation here, with nothing to take his mind off the subject, had made matters worse. She could imagine that his parents had given him everything he wanted as a child. Wealthy, indulgent parents showering him with material possessions must have left him with the impression that he only had to reach out for what he wanted to have it fall into his hands. The women he had met had only confirmed his impression. Given everything, he valued nothing.

Growing up as she had in financial security without love, Deborah had learnt to value love above everything else. For a long time she had equated it with security. Now she knew the only security lay in love, rather than the other way around. It was giving love which enriched life. She yearned to pour out her love to Alex. She had never known love in her life before. It was new-minted and precious to her, and she felt she bore an amazing present which she longed to give him, but she dared not, because what seemed so rich and splendid to her might seem pointless to him. Women had given him their love in the past, and he had dropped it carelessly. He had been showered with so much love, while she had had none. She knew it would destroy her if the chill fingers of disillusion, indifference and carelessness touched what she now had. It would be better to leave him never knowing how she felt. She might then retain the capacity to love. If she accepted the desire he offered her as a substitute for the emotion she needed, one day he would grow bored with her, and then she might be too scarred and bitter to recognise or accept any other love which she met. If she never saw Alex after they returned to London she might one day forget him, and the chance of love might return with another man.

Pausing, wiping her hot face with dusty fingers, she thought wryly: not Robin, though. He was a nice man. She liked him. But she knew now the difference between affection and passion, and it was passion she wanted, although only if it came with love. The passion Alex offered was almost impersonal. He did not know the woman behind the body he desired. Although they had worked together for so long their talk had always been of the job they did, shop talk, unadulterated by anything outside. He had rarely mentioned his family. Gossip had told her he had few relatives apart from a mother he rarely saw. What did he do in his leisure hours apart from chase women? She paused, frowning. She really knew as little about his life as he did about hers. Yet she knew with total certainty that she loved him—spoilt, egotistic, arrogant, demanding though he was, she loved him.

'Aren't you ever going to stop?' he asked at that moment from the doorway, leaning there staring around the room. 'Good heavens! Mother won't recognise it. What enormous numbers of books! I never noticed them before.'

'They were hidden under the junk,' she said, her back aching as she straightened.

'You'll be able to read instead of having to talk to me,' he said disagreeably. 'I'm hungry. Aren't you cooking any lunch?'

'I'd forgotten,' she said with a sigh, realising she had worked for hours. 'I'll wash and cook something. I'm sorry.'

Alex looked at her intently. 'You're tired,' he said more gently. 'Silly little fool, you've worn yourself out. I'll cook the lunch. You wash and then sit down for half an hour while I sort things out.'

'It's all right,' she protested, 'I can manage.'

He gripped her arm, shaking her slightly. 'Don't argue, Deb, there's a good girl. Do as you're told.'

She met the commanding eyes, sighed and acquiesced. When she had slowly washed she sat down beside the fire and watched him opening tins and moving about. He was slow but methodical. It began to make her tingle with frustration, realising he had to work out each move before he made it, unused to such work. At last they settled down to eat a delicious consommé from a tin, followed by the tinned ham served with an odd mixture of halved peaches and scrambled eggs. Replete and warm, Deborah congratulated him. She was seated in the chair, he had taken a position on the pillow at her feet.

'I'll do the washing up later,' he said, stretching his arms above his head.

'I'll do it,' she said quickly.

'No!' He turned his head and looked up at her in determination. 'I will, and no argument. But just now I'm feeling too sleepy and lazy.' He leaned backward until his head lay against her lap. 'It must be the fire,' he said, as casually as if he was unaware of the intimacy of their positions. 'I'm used to central heating, I suppose. There's something so cosy about a real fire.' She heard him yawn. 'We had rather a disturbed night, too.'

'Lie down on the bed and go to sleep for a while,' she suggested, struggling with a desire to stroke the dark head pillowed in her lap.

'I prefer to stay where I am,' he said smoothly. 'Unless you join me on the bed.'

She stiffened. 'Alex! Stop saying things like that.'

He groaned. 'No sense of humour, that's your trouble. Very well, tell me about your school. Did you like it?'

'Nobody beat me or neglected me,' she said. 'But I didn't exactly love the place.'

'Did you make many friends?'

'A few, but none I kept when I left.' Her voice quivered slightly. 'There was no one who mattered.'

'Were you very lonely as a child, Deb?'

'Yes,' she admitted. 'Were you?'

Alex turned his head and again she saw his face inverted, the silvery eyes half hidden by drooping lids. 'Oddly enough, I was. Mother had a strong belief in the importance of individual privacy, which in practice meant she showed no curiosity about my life. It's admirable in its way, but I always felt she never really cared, although with my rational mind I knew she was very fond of me. My father was always busy. I had no brothers or sisters. Like you, I went to boarding school, but I did make friends there, friends I've kept ever since. I still see one or two at times. We exchange Christmas cards, meet when we remember. But I was lonely. It's hard to pin down why, because I had everything I could wish for ...' He shrugged.

Deborah made no reply. She felt curiously sad. She

suspected Alex had been given as little love as she had, although on the surface he had been surrounded by care. Perhaps if he had not been brought up so carefully he might have been able to value love.

He turned his face towards the fire. His lids drooped altogether, protecting his eyes from the firelight. His face smoothed out into sleep. After a long silence, guessing he was unable to feel it, she allowed herself to touch his hair. Her fingers softly brushed along the back of his head, then winnowed the dark strands, letting them fall through her grasp. She leaned back, staring into the fire, her hands gently stroking his head.

The room gradually grew dusky. The bright spring sky paled. A chill began to fall as the wood burnt to ashes and the fire began to fade. Deborah dared not move for fear of waking him. There was a fierce delight in sitting here while he slept against her, unaware of her, his cheek against her knee. The moments drifted by preciously. She did not want to end them.

The sound of ash dropping through the grate woke him suddenly. He made a peculiar snorting sound, his head shifting, then she felt him tense as he realised where he was, and he turned to look at her, eyes blinking from sleep.

'My God! Why did you let me sleep on like that?' He sat up and made a face over the remains of the fire. 'You've let it go out! Have you no sense? We'll freeze to death without some warmth in this room.' He knelt beside the hearth, raking carefully, blowing some life back into what remained of the fire, feeding twigs on to it carefully until it blazed back into life.

'You must have been a boy scout,' she teased.

Alex grimaced. 'Not me!' He stretched, yawning. The movement brought awareness back to her. She looked at his lean back, the slim hips and well-shaped head. He turned and she looked away, flushing.

'Thank you for letting me sleep,' he said softly.

'How's your cold?' she asked casually.

'I think it was a figment of your imagination,' he said lightly. 'A few sneezes don't make a cold. I shall be able to sleep in the studio tonight, don't worry.'

'Don't be stupid, Alex,' she said flatly. 'There's no fire and it's bitterly cold in there. I'm not afraid you'll take advantage of me if you sleep in the same bed.'

He turned a suddenly savage face on her. 'Then you should be, because I might. I don't take your confidence in me as a compliment. I've never believed in knights in shining armour, and nor should you.'

'I don't imagine you are a knight in shining armour,' she said crisply. 'But I doubt if you enjoy rape, and it would have to be that, Alex. So there's no problem.'

He looked at her broodingly. 'You're tempting providence, Deb. Are you going to tell Robin about this? Do you think he would see it in the same light?'

'Why not?'

'Because I think Robin would prefer me to freeze to death in the studio rather than sleep with you,' he said grimly. He stared at her unsmilingly. 'If I sleep in here, I'll sleep on the floor by the fire. Then I'll be warm enough, won't I?'

She looked at him through her lashes. 'Are you a knight in shining armour, after all, Alex?' she asked him teasingly.

His face tightened. 'No,' he said in a furious voice. 'I'm a man who knows that if he has you in his bed tonight no power on earth will stop him taking you.'

Heat seemed to flame over her body. They stared at each other. She swallowed and forced herself to look away. Huskily, she said, 'Then you'd better sleep on the floor.'

'You made me spell it out for you, Deb,' he said in a tone harsh with anger. 'Now, I'd better do that damned washing up before we start cooking our evening meal. We're running out of edible supplies. Eggs again, I suppose.'

'The chickens!' she said, remembering them.

He grinned at her, his face softening. 'While you were working in the studio I spotted from the window that they'd settled on the garden wall. There are nooks and crannies in the stone. They seem to have made themselves quite comfortable. I've no doubt any eggs they've laid will be secreted among the shrubs out of sight. We'll never find them—hens have a genius for laying eggs where you can't find them.'

'How do you know about hens?' she asked him.

'I've stayed here,' he said, beginning to sort out the washing up to carry it into the bathroom.

Deborah tidied the room and began to find the eggs and the rest of the ham, intending to make them omelettes for supper. Alex came back while she was beating the eggs and deposited the clean crockery on the small table they were using. She had discovered it in the studio and although it was rickety and very stained with paint it was serviceable.

'The flood water is definitely going down,' he told her. 'Tomorrow we'll tackle the water in the house. It will have to be swept out—there are yard brooms in one of the sheds.'

'Goodness knows what sort of mess the room downstairs will be in,' she said, grimacing. 'It will have to be scrubbed thoroughly, and even then that river smell will hang around for days. We must open all the windows and doors to air the place. You must light fires, too, Alex.'

He was standing staring at her with a fixed expression. She turned, sensing tension between them, and met his eyes with puzzled enquiry.

'Are you trying to domesticate me, Deb?' he asked.

Her eyes widened. 'If you don't want to help me, don't.' Her voice hardened with resentment. 'It's your mother's house, not mine.'

Alex stared a moment longer, then his lips twisted wryly. 'I'm sorry. You're right, it has to be done. I suppose the task seems so formidable that I dread the idea.'

'It will be hard work,' she said, nodding. 'But it has to be done. It would be dreadful for your mother to come back and find her house ankle-deep in mud.'

'I hope she's suitably grateful to you,' he said drily.

Deborah resented the remark. 'I'm not asking for gratitude. Anyone would do the same.'

All the time she had been making the supper. Now she slid two golden omelettes on to warmed plates while he watched her, his expression ironic.

'You're a superb cook, aren't you, Deb?' he asked in a voice which was far from pleasant. 'Perfectly shaped, perfectly risen omelettes cooked on a grotty old stove in impossible conditions ... what an ideal wife you're going to make! I hope Robin appreciates his good fortune.'

She handed him his plate with a slap, thrusting it into his hands, then sat down on the pillow by the fire and ate her own, her head averted from him. The meal progressed in silence. Afterwards, they washed up in silence and tidied the room, avoiding each other's eyes.

Deborah spent five minutes in the bathroom, returning in the white smock to climb into bed. Alex watched her walk across the room with grimly narrowed eyes. During her absence he had spread his bedclothes close to the fire.

He went out. She had sorted out several books from the pile she had found in the studio, and she opened one and looked through it listlessly. It was a Victorian cookery book, French, each page having a small illustration of a recipe, and although she was amused and fascinated by the incredible quantities suggested for the dishes, her mind could not concentrate on what she read.

They had run out of eggs. Would they be able to find any tomorrow? The alarms over the storm and following flooding might have made the hens stop laying. Her mouth was dry. She longed with physical eagerness for a cup of tea. The very thought of it made her groan. Since they arrived she had drunk only water, and the three bottles of Vichy water Alex had discovered had now all gone. Tomorrow they would have to think seriously about the problem of drinking water. If the water had subsided there might be traffic along the road. They had seen none all day, and she suspected the road was little used even in dry weather. But surely some vehicle must pass soon.

Alex came back wearing the black silk dressing-gown. Deborah looked at him through her lowered lashes, aching with love. 'If a car comes past tomorrow you could get a lift into the village and get help,' she said huskily.

He nodded. 'I don't know if a car is likely to pass, but a barge may come along. I've kept my eyes open now and then, but I've seen nothing.'

'A barge?' she frowned.

'Flat-bottomed barges pass along the river—they still use them around here to transport goods. If the road seems passable I'll walk to the village, though.'

'No,' she said emphatically. 'It would make your cold worse again. Why don't I go? If I follow the road I'm bound to find a village.'

Alex gave her an irritated look. 'Don't be absurd. If anyone goes I will!'

'Then we'll stay here,' she said obstinately. She did not like the idea of being left alone in this isolated house in a foreign country.

He made no answer, sliding down between his bedclothes until only the dark sheath of his hair was visible. His head was turned facing the fire. She hesitated, nervously probing her lip with her tongue.

'I was going to read, but if you want to sleep...'

'Read for as long as you like,' he said tersely.

Tears pricked at her eyes. His hostile tone hurt and she felt wearily miserable. She closed the book and let it slide to the floor, then leaned over to turn down the paraffin lamp. Darkness settled over the room, leaving only the banked-up glow of the fire to illuminate it.

She lay on her face, burying herself in her pillow, silently crying without being able to halt the tears. They soaked into her pillow, making her face wet.

She heard Alex make a harsh sound, and heard him move. Alarm held her still, tensing to guess what he was doing. He couldn't have heard anything; she knew she had not made a sound. But he padded over to the bed on bare feet and sat down beside her, his hand suddenly curving around the loose blonde hair.

'I'm sorry if I snapped,' he said gently.

Unable to reply, she nodded faintly, knowing he would feel the movement under his hand.

'For God's sake, don't cry,' he said in abrupt harshness.

She lay immobile, surprised. How had he known? Had she after all betrayed herself by some sound? The long hard fingers moved caressingly over her hair, stroking her head in a tender movement.

She forced herself to speak, to reassure him. 'I'm all right,' she said brightly.

For a few seconds Alex didn't move, then his hands picked her up by her still quivering shoulders and turned her over to face him. The firelight made a dim red glow by which they looked at each other. His fingers softly drew across her wet lashes, then ran down her face, tenderly wiping away the tearstains. She sighed, content seeping into her. Alex groaned. His mouth lowered and trailed over her closed eyes, softly caressed the damp curves of cheek and mouth, lingering without passion, their hard outline warm as they parted her lips.

'Everything will be fine tomorrow,' he said soothingly. 'I promise you. Someone will come past and by tomorrow night you'll be safely back in Nice to catch the plane home.'

'Yes,' she sighed, snuggling down under her bedclothes.

Alex looked down at her, hesitated, then bent and kissed her again, still without passion, yet with a tenderness which made her tremble. Deborah returned the kiss softly, but her response brought a deepening pressure which made her heart turn over. Without volition her hands moved up to encircle his head and she lifted her face, her lips parting hungrily. Alex made a soft sound, gripping her, his hands sliding under her back. They moved together, holding each other, kissing in a totally new way. Alex suddenly broke away, his breath audible in the quiet room.

'I can't take much more of this,' he said hoarsely, and got up, striding back to his own makeshift bed to vanish between the bedclothes. With a faint smile on her mouth Deborah drifted gently into sleep. Alex had offered her hunger, desire, violence, many times before, but for the first time there had been a totally new feeling in his kiss.

CHAPTER EIGHT

NEXT day after a breakfast of baked beans and boiled water they ventured downstairs and found that most of the water had seeped away, leaving a thin covering of mud everywhere and an appalling smell of the river, a rotten odour which pervaded every room. They had rolled up their jeans, but there had been nothing they could do about their footwear since they had only the shoes they wore when they arrived, which were not the most suitable objects for wading in muddy water.

Alex found two stiff yard brooms and they began to work, sweeping the water systematically out of the house. Every now and then they halted, perspiring, their legs plastered with mud, saturated with water. It was tiring physical work. After half an hour Alex pulled off his shirt and worked with his lean chest bare, the muscles rippling across his arms and back as he swept vigorously. Deborah envied him. It was impossible for her to imitate him.

'I should have brought my bikini,' she groaned, wiping her face with one hand, the sweat running down her back, making her top stick to her.

'It would certainly have made the work more enjoyable for me,' he agreed, teasingly, then turned to grin at her, and roared with laughter.

'What's funny?' she asked, taken aback.

'If you could see yourself! I never expected to see the perfectly groomed, cool as a cucumber Miss Portman working ankle deep in mud, her clothes crumpled, her face smeared with mud ...'

She began to laugh in response, eyeing him. 'You

don't look any more elegant yourself,' she pointed out.

He grimaced. 'I know. I feel as though I've been wearing these clothes for a week.' He wrinkled his nose. 'I wouldn't mind the work. The smell is the worst—the house will reek for weeks. Mother will have to have the whole place redecorated. Look at that wallpaper ... the water level has left a black tide mark all round the house ...'

'I'm afraid your mother is in for a shock,' she said in concern.

Alex shrugged. 'I doubt it. I remember her telling me these floods occur at regular intervals. She probably expects it, which is why she removed all her furniture from the downstairs rooms. She must have had a van from the village to take them. There wouldn't have been room for them in the bedroom.'

'And I doubt if she could have got so much as a jam-jar into that studio,' said Deborah, remembering the mess she had found. 'I think your mother is a squirrel. She seems to keep the oddest things ... old newspapers, jigsaw puzzles ...'

'Newspapers,' said Alex abruptly.

She stared at him. 'What about them?'

'We could use them to dry the floor when we've swept out the water.'

'That's a good idea,' she agreed enthusiastically. 'The floorboards will take ages to dry out.'

Alex recommenced sweeping, his hard lean body bent as he pushed the filthy water towards the open door. Deborah worked beside him, her blonde hair tied up into a loose knot at the back of her head. Her top was sticking to her and her muscles were aching.

They worked until all the water was clear of the house. Alex ran up to get the pile of newspapers and they carefully distributed them around the rooms. The mud soaked through immediately, turning the yellowing pages grey. Although they had left all doors and windows open there was a sweet-rotten graveyard smell to the house which filled the nostrils unpleasantly.

'I'll go and see if I can find any eggs,' Alex said.

'I'll come with you,' Deborah replied quickly.

He looked at her in surprise, searching her face. 'Afraid I'll vanish, Deb?' The question was gently teasing.

'I want to breathe clean air,' she told him frankly.

He made a face. 'I know what you mean.'

The long garden was vividly green, as if the flood waters had given it new life. The ground sloped upward behind the house so the deluge had been far less as it swept through the garden and it had soaked away much more quickly. Vegetables grew in neat rows along one side. Fruit trees clustered at the far end in the shelter of a crumbling old stone wall. As they walked slowly, breathing the sweet morning air, Deborah's eyes dwelt on the expanse of snowy white blossom which stretched on either hand as far as the eye could see. The orchards fluttered softly in a faint breeze, their branches trembling gently. Every now and then a few petals blew away, filling the blue sky with delicate fragility, as if it spawned snowflakes.

'It seems a hundred years since I walked outside the house,' she said, smiling. 'Yet we've only been shut up there for a short time. Have you ever noticed how time has a habit of telescoping? Sometimes it goes too slowly, sometimes too fast.'

'And since we've been here it's been going too slowly, has it, Deb?' Alex asked in a sharpening tone.

She looked at him sideways. 'That wasn't intended as a nasty remark. Just that ... so much has happened in the past two days, I seem to have forgotten what the world outside looks like.'

'Even Robin?' he asked sardonically.

She sighed wearily. 'Don't, Alex!'

He grimaced. 'Sorry.' The word was muttered aside, his head averted. He lifted his eyes along the stone wall. It was obviously very old, the stone mellowed to a warm patina of grey and yellow, hollowed in places, forming mini-caves which at this moment held a few contentedly roosting hens, their beady eyes observing the two humans suspiciously. One stretched out her neck, uttering a quavering cry of hostility, her red comb trembling. The others joined in the chorus, shivering their feathers as though hoping it would drive the intruders away. Others strutted to and fro among the long muddy grass along the wall, bending to search for insects, their gawky forms stiffly proceeding, like aldermen at a city banquet.

'We'll look under the nesting ones first,' said Alex, firmly shifting a protesting hen and groping beneath her warm body. She pecked at him ferociously, squawking. He made a furious noise, sucking his wrist, but he had found an egg, and exhibited it triumphantly.

Deborah felt an odd reluctance to follow suit. She eyed the nearest hen, swallowing, then tentatively tried to push her hand beneath the soft feathered body.

'Three so far,' said Alex, pleased with himself, then turned to look at her as she fumbled around, her hand jerking away whenever the hen viciously pecked at her.

His laughter made her flush crossly. 'Their beaks hurt,' she said, scowling at him.

'You have to be bold,' he explained, coming over to her. 'Hens are females. They respond to a firm, commanding hand.' His silvery eyes glinted sardonically at her. 'They have to be shown who's master.'

She made a face at him. 'Show-off ... you're used to the damned things, you find her egg. I don't even want it any more.' She licked the blood from her nipped hand and wrist irritably. 'That creature is spiteful.' She gave the hen a ferocious look. 'One day you'll end up as coq au vin and serve you right, you horrible bird!'

Alex grinned, eyes twinkling. Smoothly he slid a hand beneath the hen, his other hand holding her head so that she could not peck him. His palm uncurled under Deborah's nose, exhibiting a speckled brown egg. 'You just have to know how to treat females,' he said tauntingly.

Sulkily, she said, 'Well, there's another one nesting in the apple tree over there and she has a broody look in her eyes. You'd better climb up and rescue whatever she's sitting on, hadn't you, master-mind?'

He laid the fourth egg alongside the others he had found, on a nest of damp grass on a bird table. She watched as he deftly swarmed up the knobbly bole of the tree and hooked himself on to a safe foothold before reaching under the small, brown bridling hen. She watched him, beady eyes intent, then suddenly flew up, wings feathering the air.

Alex was startled by her attack into leaning backwards. His feet slipped and he fell heavily out of the tree, giving a cry of irritated alarm. Deborah ran to him, her face white with anxiety.

Kneeling, she bent over him, asking hurriedly, 'Alex, are you hurt? Are you all right?'

He was lying spreadeagled, his head cushioned on long wet grass, groaning. The sunlight filtering through the branches of the apple tree fell in a speckled pattern over his face. A few white petals fluttered from the blossom-heavy branches and lay against his brown chest.

'Alex, say something!' she begged, agonised, his silence making her afraid he had injured himself badly.

'Bloody hen,' he muttered suddenly, opening his eyes, his face furious.

'Where does it hurt?' she asked, carefully beginning

to feel his shoulders and arms. 'You haven't broken anything?'

He jackknifed into a sitting position. 'No,' he said. 'No, I'm in one piece, no thanks to that feathered assassin.'

Deborah began to laugh, half in amusement, half in deep relief, and he eyed her smoulderingly.

'I don't see what's funny.'

She mocked him, her blue eyes bright, the sunlight falling through the branches turning her hair to fine gold. 'Who said hens need to be shown who's master? What happened to the bold, commanding hand, Alex?' Her laughter brimmed over, her mouth curving.

He gave her a dangerous look, his eyes menacing. 'I don't like being made fun of, Deb ... I didn't expect the stupid bird to do anything like that.'

'No sense of humour, that's your trouble,' she said, as he had said to her earlier. She rose to her feet. 'I'll find some more eggs while you rest here, you poor little injured soldier.'

His hand caught her ankle and jerked her off balance. She fell, crying in surprise and alarm, and was received against the wall of his bare brown chest. Dazedly her eyes looked into his at close quarters.

'Don't tease me unless you're prepared to take the consequences,' he warned softly, holding her with one arm around her back.

Tensely, she struggled to get up. Alex suddenly let her go and she fell backward, sliding on to the ground beside him, her chest heaving with the exertion of the struggle.

Alex turned, supporting himself on one elbow, watching her. She was breathing unsteadily. As her body moved in order that she might get up again, the material of her top stretched and her taut nipples were clearly visible. Alex's breath caught in his throat. One hand clamped down on the curve of her jean-clad thigh, anchoring her. Deborah looked at him in swift apprehension. Seeing the way his eyes were fixed on her she froze.

'No, Alex,' she stammered. 'Don't...' Her voice held pleading, alarm, a thread of shivering excitement.

Remorselessly his hand slid upward, pushing beneath the top, until it closed on the yielding softness of her breast. Staring at her with fever-bright eyes, he whispered, 'Deb...'

She was weakened by her own need to have him touch her. One moment there had been laughter and light companionship, the next she had felt passion flare, as storm broke in a blue sky, and she had been taken off balance, not expecting it.

His thumb moved, stroking her nipple, sending a shiver of fierce pleasure down her whole body. She felt suddenly unable to fight him any longer. Her eyes closed. Her lips trembled.

Alex made a hoarse sound and rolled over on top of her, pushing her down against the wet grass, the sweet fresh smell of the countryside all around them. As the weight of his body came down on her she could not hold back a groan of satisfaction which seemed to come from the pit of her stomach. Whether he loved her or not at that moment that forceful contact seemed utterly natural, completing her, as if until that instant she had never been whole.

Hungrily his mouth explored her parted lips, making them quiver in eager response. His tongue groaned her name pleadingly, his hands silkily wandering beneath her top, leaving fiery heat wherever they touched. She touched his bare chest, her hands possessive, shaping the tense muscles beneath her fingers, hearing a ringing in her ears, as though blood beat there, deafening her.

Alex was breathing harshly, kissing her harder. Suddenly he pushed back her top and jerked her upward until their naked bodies strained against each other as if they tried to become one form.

Her physical responses had become so overwhelming that she was terrified of the fire burning deep inside her body. She moaned, burying her face on his shoulder. 'No, Alex ...'

He pushed her away so that he could look into her face. They stared at each other. He did not say a word, but against her lower limbs his body hardened in intolerable desire, forcing her to feel the urgency of his need to possess her. The silvery eyes bored into hers, asking the question his body was demanding more potently. Deborah looked back helplessly, trembling, breathing raggedly, no longer able to find either the power or the desire to fight him any more.

His hand slowly trailed down her and began to unzip her jeans, his eyes still holding her gaze. She knew he was silently making it clear that she could stop him if she wanted to, but she could neither move nor speak, waiting in vanquished passivity for him. When she felt his hand against the warm flesh beneath her jeans she sighed, closing her eyes in wordless consent, making it clear to him that she would not deny him now.

'Oh, God,' he whispered, his voice shaking. 'Deb, Deb ...' His face buried itself in her throat, his lips trembling against her skin.

'Take me,' she moaned through lips swollen with desire, her voice barely audible. 'Alex, take me ...'

His heart pounded like a tilt-hammer above her as he sought her mouth, lowering her to the grass again, one hand tenderly soothing back the tumbled blonde hair from around her face. 'I've got to,' he said shakily. 'Hate me afterwards, but I've got to ...'

As he broke off the kiss, taking a shuddering breath, she said tenderly, 'I won't hate you, Alex.'

His eyes widened, piercing the shining blue depths

of hers. She saw the astonishment, the disbelief, the question in his stare. They were silent, enclosed in a warm golden world which held them at its heart as if they were trapped in amber, aware only of each other.

Then into the silence of that intense concentration the sound of raised voices broke in upon them like the roll of thunder on a humid day.

Alex lifted his head dazedly. His intent expression broke up. His mouth parted, grimacing. He swore savagely. Deborah felt anguish, as though she had been far away in halcyon isolation, and was being dragged back to grim reality.

'Oh, God,' she muttered, awaking to the garden, the sunlight, the knowledge of what had happened.

Alex gave her a searching, hard look. Then he rose, his head averted from her as she pulled down her top with trembling hands, her face scarlet with shame and humiliation. He moved back towards the house, and she scrambled to her feet, adjusting her clothes with fingers that trembled. Her legs seemed boneless. She could hardly walk. She had offered herself to Alex shamelessly, even failing to disguise the fact that she loved him. He must have seen it, recognised it. Had they not been interrupted she would have ... she broke off the thought with a shudder. She had so nearly become his mistress the realisation worked in her flesh like a poisoned thorn. Even though he had offered her a new, gentle tenderness at times, she knew he still did not love her, and to let him possess her without love would have been a bitter experience. Only her own aching need of him had forced her surrender. Now she hated herself for it and wished hopelessly that it had never happened.

She collected the eggs automatically and followed him into the house.

He was standing in the kitchen facing a very small,

thin erect woman in a black dress. 'Mother!' she heard him say. 'Where on earth have you been?'

Over his shoulder Deborah met a pair of searching, curious, cooling grey eyes which reminded her strongly of Alex. 'I told you on the telephone that I was moving into the village because of flood warnings,' said a clear firm voice.

'The line was so bad I only heard enough to know something was wrong,' he said, shrugging, 'so I came to find out what was going on and walked into a flood.'

Judging by her ironic expression, his mother did not believe a word. She gave a tight little smile. 'I could hear you perfectly well. Odd.'

Deborah watched dark red flood up the back of Alex's neck. He made an irritable, impatient gesture. 'I wouldn't have come if I'd known,' he snapped. 'The flood marooned us upstairs all day yesterday. We were even afraid to drink the water in case it was contaminated.'

'Poor Alex,' said his mother softly. She glanced at Deborah, who was hovering uncertainly behind him, her hands full of eggs. 'Aren't you going to introduce us?' Deborah put down the eggs quickly.

Alex swivelled, his glance not quite meeting Deborah's eyes, as though he were deeply embarrassed. 'Mother, this is Deborah Portman.'

Mrs St James looked at her with opening eyes, her face full of sudden interest. 'Your secretary?' She held out a hand, smiling. 'I'm glad to meet you at last, my dear. I've heard about you.' As Deborah took her hand, smiling back nervously, the older woman's grey eyes ran down over her in curious, amused surmise. 'Although I must say I would never have known you from the descriptions I've had of you.'

Deborah glanced at Alex, wondering what he had said about her. Mrs St James laughed, seeing the look.

'My son described a soignée, aloof swan. You're very beautiful, my dear, but I'm afraid your feathers are a little bedraggled. It must have been a terrible experience for you. A flood can be frightening. I've no doubt you'll be very relieved to get back to civilisation.'

Alex's face was brooding. 'Deb and I have swept all the water out of the house. When the newspapers dry we'll scrub the place for you,' he said. He glanced at Deborah, still not quite meeting her eyes. 'There's no need for you to hurry back, is there?' His voice was cool. 'The weekend will be finished by the time we get back to London now.'

Mrs St James watched them both intently.

Deborah looked at Alex fleetingly, then looked at her hands, linked at her waist. 'I shall be glad to help get the house straight,' she said.

'You're a very kind girl,' Mrs St James said pleasantly. 'Having seen what the place looks like, I'm doubly grateful for all you've done and for your proposal to help even further, but I've brought several women from the village with me to do all that. I expected to find the job much worse than it is, thanks to you. I shall be staying here tonight, you see. There's so little room ...' Her eyes remained pleasant, but suddenly hot red colour flooded into Deborah's face, as she realised that Alex's mother must know that she had shared a room with Alex for two nights. No doubt, knowing his usual way with women, Mrs St James imagined they were lovers.

Hearing her faint intake of breath, Alex looked round at her sharply, his eyes taking in her shamed expression. A grim look came into his face. He turned and said crisply to his mother, 'I slept on the floor of your room while Deb took the bed,' and his eyes bored into the grey ones which were so like his own, a hard insistence in them.

Mrs St James surveyed him thoughtfully, a slight frown creasing her forehead. 'I should think you did, my dear.'

Hurriedly, to change the subject, Deborah said apologetically, 'I was so bored I'm afraid I took the liberty of tidying your studio, Mrs St James. I tried not to move anything essential, but I cleared the floor space and made piles of everything.'

The older woman's eyebrows rose steeply. She looked at Alex, as if astonished, and he smiled twistedly. 'Deb has a passion for creating order out of chaos, Mother,' he said. 'She can't bear loose ends.'

Nervously, Deborah said, 'I'm sorry. Alex did warn me you preferred to have things left as they were...'

'Come and show me, my dear,' invited Mrs St James. Deborah slowly moved towards the stairs. Alex made to follow the two women, but his mother said, 'Alex dear, it was kind of you to free the hens in case they got drowned, but would you please shut them up again before they get into the orchards? Jacques Mareau will have them in his pot before I have a chance to stop him.' Her cool, quiet pleasant voice had a firm ring to it which Deborah realised, with amusement, made Alex obey without argument when it gave an order.

In the studio Mrs St James glanced slowly around the room, her eyes expressionless. Deborah fidgeted anxiously. 'I'm sorry,' she burst out, afraid she had seriously offended.

'My dear girl, I'm amazed and impressed,' Mrs St James told her. 'You've unearthed several valuable finds which I've been hunting for for months...' Her hand lifted a cracked red-brown earthenware pot and fingered it lovingly. 'So that's where it was!' She saw Deborah's look of surprise and smiled charmingly. 'I want to use it for a still life of onions, courgettes and red peppers. I knew it was somewhere here. Thank you.'

She moved across the room and picked up the portrait of Alex.

Deborah felt her face tense and glaze with hard colour. Mrs St James stared at it for some time in silence. 'He's an odd mixture,' she said softly. 'Even as a little boy he was very tough, very independent but touchingly vulnerable. When he fell over he would never cry, even when it hurt. But if I picked him up and kissed him when he fell over he would look as if he was going to cry badly.' She sighed.

Putting down the portrait, she said quietly, 'You're in love with him?'

Deborah said nothing, her throat dry with nerves.

Mrs St James turned round and looked at her directly. 'I know Alex very well. He never confides in me, but I've known him since he was a baby, and I can feel it when something is happening. I've had that feeling ever since I saw you two together. Will you tell me? Or am I being a nosy old woman?' She smiled, her thin dark face curiously reminiscent of Alex. She had his hair, the colour faded to a silvery grey which almost matched her eyes. She had a quality of quiet serenity which was impressive. Remembering what Alex had said about his mother's belief in privacy, Deborah could imagine that her reserved manner might have seemed cold to a small child, although she was sure Mrs St James loved her son deeply. Her way of talking about him indicated as much.

Moistening her lips, she said, 'There's nothing to talk about. Nothing I can say.'

Mrs St James smiled wryly. 'You prefer not to tell me?'

'No!' Deborah spoke certainly. 'But ...' She shrugged. Huskily, she said after a pause, 'To put it simply, I do love him, but he doesn't love me.' Her face reflected her humiliation as she put it so bluntly.

His mother looked at her gently. Lowering her eyes,

she asked, 'He's asked you to sleep with him, though, I suppose?'

Deborah made a low, shamed sound of astonishment.

'Oh, my dear, I've always known Alex was no angel. I read newspapers too, you know. Mind you, I've taken it all with a pinch of salt. Alex has too much of my own nature to enjoy the sort of promiscuity gossip would credit him with, and although I imagine there've been some women in his life I suspect most of his publicised affairs have been all smoke and no fire.' She laughed, her eyes twinkling. 'Men always like to be thought of as sophisticated seducers. I suppose it's the remnant of a race memory of man the hunter.'

Deborah stared at the floor. 'I'm not his mistress, Mrs St James.'

'I knew that,' his mother said softly, 'the moment I saw the two of you together. Alex was in a frightful temper and ready to bite if anyone gave him the chance. I saw something was eating at him, and when I set eyes on you I knew what it was.'

Deborah shrugged helplessly. 'After we get back to London I won't see him again. I shall leave my job and get another one.'

'I see,' said Mrs St James slowly. 'If you stayed don't you think it might not be better?'

Deborah shook her head, staring at the floor. 'I've got to get away from him. I might stop saying no and I ...' Her voice failed. 'When he asked me to marry him I almost said yes until I realised what hell it would be to love a man who didn't love me but who was my husband.'

Mrs St James made a low sound of satisfaction. 'He asked you to marry him? Congratulations! To my knowledge it's the first time.'

Deborah sighed heavily. 'But he doesn't love me. I had to refuse.'

Mrs St James looked at her pityingly. 'Deborah, I

understand how you feel, but if you could bring yourself to marry him I would be very grateful to you. Alex doesn't know it, but he's not happy. He's rootless and permanently searching for happiness he never finds. A warm, loving marriage might solve the problem.'

Deborah looked aghast. 'No! I couldn't ... it would be hell on earth.'

'He needs someone like you,' his mother said regretfully. 'Until he feels more for someone else than he does for himself Alex will be a lost soul. He shows you more concern than I've ever known him show to anyone. When you thought I imagined you'd been sleeping with him in this house Alex looked at you in a way I've never seen him look at anyone, and he sprang to protect you angrily. I was impressed. If you belonged to him as his wife I have a feeling he would make you happy.'

Deborah pressed trembling hands to her face. 'Don't!'

Alex's voice came from the foot of the stairs. 'Deb! If we leave right away we can get a lift into Nice from the son of the man who owns the orchards. Shall I accept?'

Mrs St James looked at her pleadingly. Deborah called back huskily, 'Yes, I'm coming, Alex.'

She looked at his mother, her lower lip trembling. 'Goodbye, Mrs St James. It was nice to meet you. I hope I'll see you again some time.'

Mrs St James sighed deeply. 'Goodbye, Deborah. I'll send you the portrait of Alex if you let me have your address in England.'

Deborah looked at it longingly, closed her eyes and shook her head. 'No, thank you. I would very much have liked to have it, but I want no reminders to take away with me when I leave him.'

CHAPTER NINE

THEY drove into Nice seated uncomfortably in the back of a large, ramshackle old van which jolted violently as it swayed along the roads. The floods still lay across their path for a mile or so. The tyres swished through them, sending up jets of water on either side, but the water formed no impediment since it was shallow enough for vehicles to pass through easily now. Through the grimy windows Deborah could see the orchards, like snow against the brilliant sky, and now and then, as the van took a bend sharply she saw a brief backward glimpse of the swollen muddy river, almost yellow in its swirling passage along the green banks. Here and there branches snapped from trees during the storm swirled on the surface. Once she saw the soaked fur of some dead animal. Another time a chair floated along, already beginning to sink.

Their driver, a short dark young man in dirty blue overalls and a short-sleeved blue shirt, whistled between his teeth, occasionally shouting a remark to Alex in French. Deborah held her head averted, unwilling to meet Alex's glance. They had barely spoken since they left the cottage.

They were deposited outside their hotel by their driver, who, grinning, pocketed the money Alex handed him, and assured him that their hired car would be attended to and returned to the hire firm. They were greeted with curiosity and surprise at the hotel. Deborah was embarrassed by the stares she received. Her clothes were crumpled, muddy and dishevelled. She looked like a hippie, she thought crossly.

Tightly, Alex asked for their bill and enquired about their rooms. The manager appeared, bowing, and politely assured him with an obsequious smile that he had held their rooms, imagining that they would be returning, since Mr St James was well known in Nice and he had left his luggage.

They went to their rooms immediately. Deborah was able, at last, to shed her filthy clothes and stand naked under the cool, refreshing shower, letting her body absorb the water gratefully.

Clean, dressed in her cool blue linen dress, she brushed her wet hair until it was dry enough to wind up into a chignon. A tap on her door made her stiffen. Summoning all her reserves of courage, she told Alex to come in.

He had showered and changed too. He looked at her across the room, his face unreadable, then a smile suddenly twisted his mouth cruelly. 'Back to normal, Miss Portman? Well, at least Robin will recognise the fashion plate which greets him in the office.' His eyes mocked her. 'I'd like to be a fly on the wall when you tell him you've spent the weekend shut up in a bedroom with me, though.'

She could not control her colour, but her eyes remained cool. 'When I tell him nothing happened he'll believe me.'

'Nothing?' His cool manner broke into open savagery. Red lights flared in his eyes. 'You lying little bitch, if my mother hadn't come back ...'

'Shut up!' Her voice was trembling with shame. 'Oh, God, shut up, Alex!' She turned her back on him, covering her face with her hands, shaking.

She heard him take a step towards her, then he halted. After a moment he said harshly, 'I've rung the airport. We've just got time to have a meal before we catch a flight home.'

She nodded silently, still standing with her back to him. He waited a moment, then said, 'I'll see you in the dining-room, then. We've just got time to have a very early dinner.'

When he had gone Deborah wiped the tears from her face with shaking hands, then walked into the bathroom and washed again. For five minutes she carefully applied make-up, restoring the calm mask she wanted him to see. She finished all her packing and went downstairs without hurrying.

Alex looked impatiently at her as she sat down opposite him. They had the dining-room to themselves because it was too early for the rest of the visitors to eat. A sulky waiter came to hand her a menu, and she ordered a simple meal.

They ate in silence, almost as if they were each shut into a private world. When they had finished they collected their luggage, Alex paid the bill and they took a taxi to the airport.

The flight passed in a dream for Deborah. So much had happened since they flew in to Nice that she felt her whole life had been turned upside down. She stared blindly out of the window, the milky white cloud formations pierced with vivid blue reminding her of the orchards near the cottage, snow white against the spring sky. Alex leaned back with his eyes closed, looking grimly unapproachable. He sat up to drink several double whiskies with a determination which surprised her, since he did not drink heavily.

He insisted on taking her in his taxi from the airport, dropping her at her flat in the silence of a Sunday in London, the dark street empty except for a milk bottle rolling across the pavement pursued by a small ginger cat.

Deborah said a polite farewell, her face aloof. Alex slammed the door and leaned back without even answering. The taxi drew away and she walked shakily into the building.

Judith stared at her, eyes like saucers, as she entered the flat. 'Where on earth have you been? Deb, Robin's been like a madman. What on earth possessed you to stay away all weekend with Alex ...' Her voice died away as Deborah looked at her. 'God,' she said, appalled. 'You look terrible!'

'I'm tired,' Deborah forced herself to say, dropping her case. 'I'm going to bed, Judith.'

'Robin's been ringing all weekend,' Judith said. 'What if he rings again?'

'Tell him I'm out,' said Deborah, without caring. 'Tell him I'm dead. I don't care.'

In her bedroom she undressed like a robot and fell into bed. Sleep came as a blessed relief. She slept so deeply that when she woke she had a faint headache behind her eyes. Judith looked at her quickly when she appeared ready for work next morning.

'How do you feel?' she asked anxiously.

'I'm fine,' Deborah said curtly.

'Very well, tell me to mind my own business,' Judith said wryly.

Deborah was forced to smile, her affection for her flatmate too strong for her to shut her out.

'I'm sorry, Judith, but I've had a terrible time. Alex took me to see his mother and we got caught up in a flooding river and had to stay in the cottage all weekend. I couldn't get back.' She drank some ice-cold orange juice quickly. 'I'll be late if I don't rush. See you tonight.'

She turned to leave, when Judith said quietly, 'That's what's known as the tip of the iceberg, Deb.'

Deborah looked puzzled. 'What?'

'Your little tale,' Judith said drily. 'It's what you left out that really matters, isn't it? From the way you looked when you came in last night something catastrophic happened in Nice.'

Deborah's face twisted. 'You warned me, Judith. I should have listened.'

Judith looked hard at her. 'Do you mean he finally got to you?'

Deborah flushed. 'I didn't go to bed with him, if that's what you mean, but it was touch and go ...' Her eyes were angrily self-accusatory. 'Oh, Judith, I've made such a mess of everything! I'm hopelessly in love with him and there's no future in it, and now I've got to go and tell Robin, and how I can begin to explain I've no idea.'

Judith made a compassionate face. 'Deb, I saw this coming, but I'm sorry. Was Alex difficult?'

'Difficult?' Tenderness and wry humour turned her eyes to blue fire. 'He was bloody impossible, and but for the grace of God I would have given in to him ... you told me that if he ever found how I felt I would be in trouble ... well, I am.'

'What are you going to do about him?'

'Resign,' Deborah said despairingly. 'What else can I do? I couldn't stay, knowing how I feel, knowing that sooner or later he would coax me to give in.'

Judith looked at her, sighing. 'I suppose you're right. Just where you'll find another job that pays so well I don't know, but we could always find a cheaper flat.'

'I've got contacts in the business,' Deborah shrugged. 'I'll find something.'

She left the flat and made her way to work in bright sunshine. London was bustling as always on a Monday morning. In her mind she tried to prepare a series of speeches to say to Robin, dreading their meeting. She suspected he would think the worst, whatever she said. It was like going to the dentist, she thought. She had to face it and get it over with. When it was all over she could relax.

The girls buzzed as they saw her come in and she flushed, realising with shock that gossip had already begun to spread about the weekend. Surely to God Robin had not been talking about it in the firm?

She went into her office and automatically began her morning routine. She heard Alex's door slam and saw his shadow move across the frosted glass. Her heart turned over and she steeled herself for his summons. But before she could collect herself, he left the room again, and she relaxed. She sat down and typed out a formal note of resignation. After staring at it grimly she signed it and put it in an envelope. She went into his office and placed it on his desk. Returning to her own room, closing his door, she found Robin standing in the centre of the floor, his face rigid.

'Hello, Robin,' she said flatly.

He looked her up and down with an expression which stung. 'Why did you do it?' he asked, his voice choked with temper. 'Do you realise what a fool I looked? Was it a joke between you and that bastard St James? All those people coming to my house for the weekend, thinking our engagement was going to be announced, and you go to France to spend the weekend in bed with your lover, instead ... My God, women like you are beneath contempt!'

'Listen, Robin,' she said desperately, hearing his voice rise to a bitter peak which must be heard beyond these four walls. 'I swear to you it was an accident. There was a flood, and we couldn't get back ...'

'Do you seriously expect me to believe it? I've been a fool once, but you won't fool me again. The gossip was right, wasn't it? You're his mistress. You've always been his mistress!'

The door behind her was flung open and Alex came

into the room, his body and face tense with rage. Robin's colour rose and he looked at Alex belligerently.

'She's telling you the truth,' Alex said tightly. 'She has never been my mistress and I've never laid a finger on her. The river flooded while we were visiting my mother at a lonely cottage and we couldn't get away.'

Robin's mouth twisted unpleasantly. 'Nice try, Alex. Oh, I don't blame you. You've had women throwing themselves at you for years, and you wouldn't be human if you resisted it when Deb offered herself to you ...'

His words reminded her painfully of the moment in the sunlit garden when she had done just that, utterly oblivious of everything but Alex, and she turned away, giving a low, hoarse cry of agony.

She heard Alex move, heard a crunching impact of bone on bone, and spun round in astonishment to find Robin sprawling on his back, his hand incredulously feeling his jaw. Alex stood, fists clenched, his face black with rage. 'Get out of here,' he said thickly. 'You're finished in this firm. And you can tell your gossiping cronies out there that I've asked Deborah to marry me, not to be my mistress, and if anyone else shows her any spite or discourtesy they're finished too. Do you understand me?'

White, Robin got up, looking incredulous. He backed out of the room without another word. Deborah sank down on to her chair, dropping her face on to her hands.

Alex stood there for a moment, watching her, then he said flatly, 'I've burnt our boats, Deb. You'll have to marry me now, whether you like it or not. If you refuse, they'll all believe you're my mistress.'

'You don't want to marry me!' she said, her voice muffled by her hands.

'We get on well enough,' he said casually. 'While we were at the cottage it was fun, wasn't it? You don't find my company boring or distasteful, do you?'

She shook her head, her face still buried out of sight. She was so deeply tempted that her voice shook as she said, 'But it wouldn't work. I'm resigning, Alex. Once I've gone it will blow over and anyway, in this business who cares whether I was your mistress or not?'

'I read your resignation note,' he said casually. 'I tore it up and threw it in the wastepaper basket. When you leave here it will be when I say so, not before.'

She half laughed, half groaned. 'Don't push me around, Alex. I don't want to marry you.'

His voice hardened. 'Too bad, because you're going to have to, like it or not. If you think I'm going to have this story running around the gossip columns you're wrong ... you've got to marry me. I'll lose face if you refuse after a public announcement like that.'

She lifted her head, pushing straying blonde hair out of her eyes. 'Robin lost face and you expect him to put up with it.'

His face blackened with rage. 'I'm not Robin! You're going to marry me, Deb.'

She stood up and collected her things. 'There's no point in prolonging the argument. I'll go now. I've resigned and I'll forfeit my salary. It would be easier if I went straight away.'

Alex stared at her, the angular cheekbones forcing their way through his brown skin as he kept his temper. Cruelty tautened the wide, hard mouth. 'I should have taken you when I had the chance. Then you would have been grateful for an offer of marriage.'

The words bit home like daggers. Deborah swayed, her face losing colour. Pulling herself together, she walked out of the office and through the whispering, staring girls, her head held high, looking neither to left nor to right.

She was half afraid Alex would follow her, but she

reached the lift without an incident, and at last she was out of the building and alone.

She was too emotionally torn to go back to her flat. On impulse she took a taxi to the Zoo and walked around the enclosures, staring sightlessly at the animals, barely aware of where she was or what happened around her. Finding herself near the café, she went inside and got some coffee and sat drinking it. Time seemed to be dragging past. She was too miserable to care what she did, and as she passed a cinema an hour later, she went inside and sat through a long programme of French films, understanding nothing of what she saw on the screen, her mind unrolling for her totally different scenes which made her shiver with anguish and desire.

Remembering her life before she went to Nice, she felt she had altered totally, as if every cell in her body were changed. The cool, collected girl who had run the office so efficiently, keeping Alex firmly at bay while forming tidy plans of a pleasant future with Robin, had been a stranger she could barely recall.

In a few days Alex had wrenched her out of her formal pattern, driven her mad with love and destroyed her whole view of life. Now she had to pick up the pieces of her life and begin again, but this time, she thought wryly, with a deeper understanding of her own nature. She had made too many plans, had too many fixed ideas. She had never understood herself or her own emotions.

On the screen a thin dark girl was saying hoarsely, *'Je t'aime,'* again and again, and the words percolated to Deborah's brain suddenly, bringing a wave of heat sweeping over her body. Through the flood of her troubled emotions one fact stuck like granite piercing water—she loved Alex.

She might be made desperately unhappy by that love,

but it had shaken up the jigsaw puzzle of her life, making the pieces fit. Love could hurt deeply, even destroy, but it enriched life more than it diminished it. She would never regret having loved him. It had given her life a framework at last.

It was growing dark when she came out of the cinema, and she was very tired. She had worn her body out that morning, walking around the Zoo endlessly. This afternoon she had sat in the darkened cinema wearing out her mind with enduring the pain of loving Alex. Now she jumped on a bus and found her way back to her flat, knowing she would sleep that night. She was too tired to do anything else.

She let herself into the flat and came to a halt in alarm seeing Alex leaning back in a corner of the sofa. He looked grimly intent as they looked at each other. He was wearing a black rollneck sweater and jeans, his thick dark hair dishevelled as though he had been out in a high wind. The silvery eyes ran over her.

'Where the hell have you been all day?' he demanded jerkily. 'I was beginning to think of ringing the police.'

'Where's Judith?' she asked flatly.

'She had to go out,' he said.

She sighed. 'Did you ask her to go, Alex?'

'Yes,' he said bitingly. 'O.K., I asked her to go out. We've got to talk, Deb, like it or not.'

'We've said all we have to say,' she said, bending her head, the blonde hair falling over her slight shoulders.

'I haven't said all I have to say,' he told her, his voice growing harder.

'I don't want to hear any more,' she said wearily. 'Please, go, Alex. I'm so tired.'

He got up in a fierce movement and pushed her backward on to the sofa. Deborah sighed, leaning there, unable to move. He sat down again and looked at her, his eyes narrowed. She could feel him working out what to say next; she had seen him negotiating so many times before. She knew every subtle twist and turn of that shrewd mind.

Suddenly he said, 'You know why I want to marry you, Deb.'

She tensed. She had not expected a direct attack of this kind. She looked at him warily. 'It wouldn't work.'

'You know damned well it works,' he said thickly. 'Every time we touch each other it works.'

Her face flooded with colour. She trembled, her eyes dropping, and her hands twisted in her lap.

Alex watched her, waiting for her to answer, then said brutally, 'I could have you now and you wouldn't even stop me.'

She looked at him, then, her eyes bitterly angry. But she did not try to deny it.

His breathing quickened. 'If you're worried about other women you needn't be. I'll keep my marriage vows. There's going to be no other women.'

Her heart missed a beat, staring at him. Then her eyes clouded over and she shook her head. 'You're leaving out a vital factor, Alex.'

His eyes narrowed and a strange brooding look came into his face. 'What?' he asked tersely.

'Love,' she said simply.

He leaned back against the back of the sofa, his face unreadable. 'All right,' he said at last in cool tones. 'If you fall in love with another man after we're married, I'll give you a divorce. Will that do?'

She stared at him, half on the point of tears, half hysterical with laughter. 'You're such a fool, Alex,' she said weakly.

'I must be,' he said, his jaw hard.

'And if you fall in love I'm to give you a divorce, of course?' she asked mockingly.

'I won't,' he said with certainty.

'Oh, Alex, don't tempt fate. You can't make predictions about love,' she said sadly. 'They didn't call it the cruel god in the ancient world without reason.'

He shrugged. 'You know my views about the subject. Well, Deb, is it a bargain?'

She still hesitated, then, with a sigh, she capitulated. She might regret it bitterly later, but tonight she was too tired to run any more, and she nodded.

Alex let out a long sigh, relaxing. 'God, you strike a hard bargain, Deb. Even an escape clause. We'll get married right away. There's no point in waiting.' His eyes darkened. 'No point,' he repeated.

She trembled, seeing the look in his eyes. 'Very well,' she agreed calmly enough.

'Anyway,' he said mockingly, 'you might change your mind. The sooner the better. Where do you want to go for a honeymoon? Italy? The West Indies? Greece?'

She shrugged. 'Do we need a honeymoon? It's hardly a conventional love match.'

His face tightened. 'Don't irritate me, Deb.'

She surveyed him through her lashes. 'I'd prefer somewhere quiet and peaceful rather than a luxury hotel.' With a stir of the heart she thought of some country cottage where she could cook meals for him, wash his clothes and find his ties when he lost them.

He grinned. 'How would it do if I persuaded Mother to lend us her cottage while she had a holiday in some romantic spot? Would you like that?'

Her senses tingled. She could not meet his eyes, her mouth suddenly dry. 'Why not?' she asked huskily. 'It must be very pretty there when the weather is fine.'

'I'll ring her,' he said, rising. 'Her telephone will be working again by tonight. When I tell her we're getting married it will be the surprise of her life.' He grinned. 'I expect she'll suspect it's a joke. She could have had no idea when we were there.'

Deborah kept her eyes lowered. 'I liked your mother,'

she said. 'I hope she'll approve.'

'Of course she'll approve,' he said. He stood there, staring at her bent head. The silence between them elongated. She heard her heart beating fast. 'Kiss me, Deb,' he said, his voice suddenly rough.

She looked up at him, suddenly shy. Jerkily he bent, taking her face between both hands, and kissed her softly. Her lips parted and her eyes closed. She waited for his kiss to deepen, but after a slight hesitation he released her and moved away. He was flushed. 'Goodnight, Deb.' He walked to the door. 'For once I'll make all the arrangements, my efficient Miss Portman. I'll have to rearrange my business schedule to free myself for a fortnight. I should think we could be married next week and fly back to Nice at once.' He gave her a hard smile. 'I'll have to find another assistant, too, won't I?'

'If we're married there's no reason why I should leave,' she said in realisation.

Alex frowned. 'Damn you, my wife isn't working, especially in the same office as myself. How the hell would I get any work done?'

'And it might interfere with your flirtations with people like Sammy Starr,' she said, suddenly bitter.

His brows jerked together. 'There'll be no flirtations,' he told her bitingly. 'I gave you my word and I never break my word. Oh, go to bed, Deb. You look drained and your temper is fraying at the edge. We'll discuss things when you're less fraught.' He went out slamming the door hard.

Deborah stared at the door, sighing. She knew she had made a terrible error in agreeing to marry him, but it was done now. How was she going to bear the agony of being his wife, sharing his bed, and knowing he did not love her?

CHAPTER TEN

'ARE you pulling my leg?' Judith enquired incredulously, gazing at Deborah with great eyes. She sat down heavily, the ginger mass of her hair full and untidy as ever.

Deborah shook her head soberly. 'I'm marrying him next week,' she told her quietly.

Judith surveyed her in silence for a long moment. 'Deb, are you mad? You know only too well what sort of man he is ... you might as well keep a tiger in a cage as try to make a married man out of Alex St James!'

Deborah's mouth twisted. 'It's a chance I'm going to have to take,' she said. 'I know I'm mad. I know all the commonsense reasons why I shouldn't marry him, including the fact that I'm crazily in love with him and he doesn't even believe in love ... but I'm past caring. Even if he never loves me, even if he's unfaithful to me, I want to be his wife.' She made a self-derisive face. 'I'm too used to doing things for him, Judith. I've been his right hand for four years, and if I left I don't know if I could bear it. Being his wife is just the same, in a way. I can take care of him.'

Judith closed her eyes and groaned. 'Oh, heaven preserve us! You're a glutton for punishment. Deb, being his wife is a lot more complicated than being a mixture of housekeeper and secretary.'

Deborah's throat closed in sudden excitement and apprehension. 'I know that,' she said.

Their eyes met silently, then Judith spread her hands in a wry gesture.

'Oh, well, I hope it works out for you.' Her eyes

smiled. 'I'll have to find a new flatmate, and I doubt if I'll ever find one as easy to live with as you've been, not to mention one who likes cooking and housework.'

'I'll pay my share of the rent until you do find one,' Deborah said earnestly.

Judith laughed. 'Oh, Deb, I shall miss you ...'

'I'll be around,' said Deborah, warmed by the remark. 'You must come to visit us.' Her heart shook as she said the word. It had a deep personal significance for her. For the first time in her life she would be half of a couple, belonging to another person, and although she had contemplated marrying Robin she knew suddenly that never had that special magic of belonging ever touched their relationship.

A few days later she had just finished taking a leisurely bath, her blonde hair pinned up on top of her head, her white neck exposed in a soft sweep, when she heard a knock at the door and looked at it in surprise. She was due to go out for dinner with Alex that evening, their first real time together since she became engaged to him, hence her elaborate preparations.

Making a face, she thought: how typical of him to catch me still half dressed! He was not due for an hour. Then she realised it must be Judith coming home. She had been kept late at school that evening with a parents' meeting, but perhaps she had been able to get away before she had expected. Judith often forgot her key. She was as absentminded with that as with all her other possessions.

Opening the door, a teasing smile on her face, Deborah was stricken to silence by finding Robin on the doorstep.

He looked very attractive, in evening clothes, his expression stubborn yet filled with embarrassment.

She collected herself with an effort. 'Hallo, Robin.'

She stood in his path, making it clear she did not intend to invite him into the flat.

His pleasant hazel eyes looked pleadingly at her. 'I've got to talk to you, Deb.'

'What about?' she asked flatly.

'You know what I mean,' he said awkwardly. His jaw tightened. 'Oh, look, I jumped to disgusting conclusions about you the other day. I've come to apologise ... Deb, I was in a temper. I didn't really believe those things, I was just hurt and angry. Look, I have to explain, please ...'

She hesitated, then stood back and he came into the flat. She pulled her loose silk wrap closer around her and faced him, waiting.

Robin ran a hand through his hair. 'I'd invited young Hussey from our department to join us for the party,' he said. 'He was visiting his sister in Exeter, and as he was so close I asked him to drive over for the party. Of course, he knew about our engagement, and when you just failed to turn up without having rung or contacted me, it was bloody embarrassing.' He looked at her, remembered hurt sparking in his eyes. 'Good lord, Deb, he knew about your trip to Nice with Alex. Everyone in the office knew. I felt an idiot.' His colour deepened. 'I didn't know where to put myself.'

'I'm sorry, Robin,' she said, appalled. 'I can understand how you felt. I'm sorry, truly ... I didn't mean to hurt you ... I'm fond of you. But ...' she made a helpless gesture. 'I've fallen in love with Alex.'

Robin stared at her incredulously. 'After four years? Suddenly like that? After all you've said about him?'

'It sounds stupid, put like that,' she said, flushing. 'I can't begin to explain. I suppose I have always loved him. I just never knew before.'

Robin's colour was high. 'Deb ...' He hesitated, then stammered angrily, 'Did you and he ...'

'No,' she said, reading his mind. 'No.'

'Deb, how can you just switch like that?' He sounded more angry than hurt. 'You were getting engaged to me one minute, the next you say you're marrying him.'

'I'm sorry. I made a mistake,' she said lamely. 'I mistook my fondness for you for love.' She looked at him gently. 'I am fond of you, you know, really fond of you. But marriage takes more than that.'

'Have you got a drink?' he asked abruptly. 'I need one. I had to screw myself up to the point of coming here, and I feel terrible ...'

She went into the kitchen to find him a glass of the brandy Judith had been given by one of her boy-friends last Christmas. Robin fidgeted, loosening his tie. 'I'm hot,' he said, shedding his jacket. 'I feel pretty shaken about all this, Deb.' He took the glass and swallowed some of the brandy. 'I've had a hell of a time.'

'Have you found another job?' she asked anxiously. 'Or would you like me to speak to Alex?'

'No, I damn well wouldn't,' he said, furious. He turned away abruptly and the frill of his evening shirt caught on the corner of the kitchen cabinet, ripping, so that it dangled in a torn strip. 'Oh, damn!' he exclaimed, exasperated. 'That's all I need! I'm having dinner with a potential employer and now I shall look like a tramp!'

Deborah found herself suppressing an affectionate smile. Robin's pride, not his heart, had been hurt, she thought, or he would not be so concerned with his appearance. 'Take it off,' she said kindly. 'I'll mend it.'

He caught the look on her face and grimaced. 'I'm sorry. I sound hysterical, I know, but I've had a hell of a week ...' He took off his shirt, his back towards her, and she went into her bedroom, leaving him in the kitching finishing his brandy. Getting out her sewing machine, she repaired the frill so that the tear was invisible. She left the shirt on the bed and called Robin. He came, his glass in his hand, looking more cheerful. She hoped he had not been drinking too much if he wanted to get another job.

'You're an angel, Deb,' he said, picking up the shirt and looking at it with relief.

She heard a key in the door and went out to greet Judith, halting in surprise as she saw Alex instead. He was devastating in his formal evening clothes, his lean good looks emphasised by them. The silvery eyes looked at her lingeringly. She felt herself tremble, flushing, at the open hunger in his gaze.

'I met Judith on the doorstep talking to one of your neighbours,' he said softly. 'She told me to come up and gave me her key.' His smile was inviting. 'I think she wanted to give us a few minutes alone, and now I'm glad she did.' His eyes caressed her. 'You're quite delectable in that, Deb, even though you should be dressed by now ...' His voice died as Robin came out of the bedroom, doing up his shirt.

Slowly the grey eyes moved from Robin's flushed, defiant face to Deb's revealing, silky wrap.

The look on his face made her feel sick. Robin stood there, not speaking, a strange obstinate embarrassment in his expression. There was a moment of nightmare immobility.

'Robin tore his shirt,' said Deborah, driving herself into speech. 'I sewed it up for him.'

'I'm very grateful, Deb,' Robin said, turning to look at her, ignoring Alex. 'Thanks for everything.' He grabbed his jacket and tie and walked towards the door. 'I'll be seeing you ...' he said as he left, and every word he uttered deepened the stony harshness of Alex's gaze.

When he had gone there was a silence so intense it made ice crawl down Deborah's spine. Slowly she drew a shaky breath. Why didn't Alex say something? Why was he standing there like a frozen statue, staring at her?

At last he said through tight lips, 'You'd better get dressed for dinner.'

'Not now,' she said incoherently, trembling.

'Why not?' The question was charged with savagery. 'Too worn out by an afternoon in bed with Robin?' The question took her breath away, although she had known very well what he was thinking.

Heat flooded her face. 'No, damn you! I didn't go to bed with him. I never have.' Yet wasn't that what Robin had intended him to think? She knew Robin. His appearance had been deliberate, an attempt to get his revenge on Alex by making him think exactly what he had thought. It had been a gesture of angry pride aimed at Alex, proving that Robin had never loved her, was merely suffering from wounded self-love in losing her to Alex.

'Do you seriously expect me to believe that?' Alex's voice held bitter contempt. The grey eyes travelled over her insultingly. 'You once told me you weren't cold when Robin made love to you, and I should have believed it.'

She turned away in despair, realising he would never believe her. His view of life made it impossible for him to understand either her or the way she felt. 'Go away, Alex,' she said huskily. 'Go away.'

'Get dressed,' he commanded. 'We're going out to dinner, and in three days' time we're getting married.'

'Not now,' she said incredulously. Pain made her voice shake. 'No, Alex, I can't!'

'I've made all the arrangements,' he said in a voice as hard as granite. 'You'll marry me if I have to force you to do it. No woman is walking out on me.'

She looked at him with agony, seeing his eyes like

lakes of grey ice. His face was as impossible to read, as unyielding as a carved image. She felt suddenly terrified of him. The remote, watchful stranger facing her was implacable, dangerous.

'I can't marry you,' she said in self-protective dismay.

His mouth tightened to a thin, cruel line. 'You will,' he said, meaning every syllable. Menace emanated from him. Their eyes locked and she realised that her will power was no longer strong enough to fight against his. Her love had weakened her. She ached with misery.

'I should never have said I would marry you,' she whispered. 'Please, Alex, let me go ...'

'You're not backing out now,' he said. 'You will marry me.'

Three days later she did, very quietly, to avoid the blaze of publicity the event would otherwise cause, and they flew off to Nice the same afternoon. Alex worked on a briefcase of documents throughout the flight, only breaking off to have a drink, his manner remote and austere. Deborah sat beside him, wondering if any insanity ran in her family. She must have been out of her mind to marry him. All her doubts buzzed in her head, as they had for the last three days, but Alex's iron will power had been irresistible.

They drove to his mother's cottage in another hired car, but this time along roads made glorious by perfect weather. When the bridal white orchards came into view Deborah was disappointed to see that the blossom was fast fading now, many of the branches denuded already. It seemed an inauspicious omen.

Mrs St James had not come to the wedding. She had been busy getting the cottage ready for them, Alex had said, and her dislike of flying had made the journey to London an ordeal she really preferred not to face. Instead, she had spent the time working on the cottage, seeing her furniture returned to it, having it painted to expunge the traces of the flood waters. Now she had left for a fortnight in Paris, meaning to enjoy the opportunity to wander around the famous art galleries there, but she would return in time to spend a day with them at the cottage, she had said in a letter, as she wanted to get to know her new daughter-in-law better.

Deborah had not told Alex that she had had a private letter from his mother telling her that the marriage had made her very happy. The letter had not been meant for Alex's eyes.

Mrs St James had seen to it that everything at the house was in order for their arrival, even the kitchen range had been lit and left gently banked up for their arrival, so that it was possible to cook a meal at once. While Alex shifted their luggage upstairs and put away the car Deborah prepared a meal with the provisions her mother-in-law had carefully provided. A brief, affectionate note hidden among them raised her spirits a little, but as they later ate the meal Alex's brooding mood did nothing to lighten Deborah's heart.

She had a terrible feeling that she had just made the catastrophic error to end all errors. She had married a man who resented her.

When they had finished their meal they worked together in silence to clear away and wash up. She glanced nervously at her watch as they finished. Alex caught the look and said expressionlessly, 'You must be tired. Go to bed. I'll check everything down here.'

Without a word she went up the stairs and into the all-too-familiar bedroom. Slowly she got ready for bed. Did he intend to join her, or was he intending to sleep elsewhere? Nothing between them could indicate any warmth now. Even the fierce passion he had once offered her seemed totally dead. He was a cold, unfeeling stranger.

There was a fire burning in the grate, another example of his mother's thoughtfulness, and Deborah put out the light, standing in front of it for a while, recalling with pain the peace and gentleness which had been between herself and Alex while he slept with his head on her lap beside that fireplace. It had all gone.

She heard his foot on the stair, the creak of the floorboards, and hurriedly dived across the room into the bed, turning on to her side, pulling the bedclothes up until her head was almost buried in them, facing the wall.

She heard the door open, then quietly close. Alex stood motionless for a moment and she sensed that he was staring across the room at the bed. After a pause he began moving about. She tried to close her ears as well as her eyes, her pulses hammering.

Suddenly she heard him move beside the bed and she held her breath, trembling. He slid between the sheets and turned towards her. Ice seemed to be flowing over her body. She could not move or speak. If she lay very still, she thought desperately, he might believe she was asleep.

Silently he pulled her round to face him, his hands unkind. 'You aren't asleep,' he said coldly. She was forced to open her eyes and look at him by the red glow of the fire, his features set in that granite, unsmiling mask which had been his face ever since he saw her with Robin at the flat.

She swallowed nervously. If he touched her in this mood, if he made love to her, she knew she would die of sheer misery. His savage anger that night in Nice when he made love to her as if he wanted to kill her, forcing her body almost to the point of rape, had been less hard to bear than his present silent remoteness.

'If you want me to leave you alone you can think again,' he said harshly. 'I married you to get you into bed, and you're not cheating on that side of our bargain.'

Jerkily she whispered, 'I'm tired after the flight. It's been a long day. Not tonight, Alex, please ...' Her voice throbbed with a plea for kindness.

His mouth curled in a cruel, ironic smile. 'That old feminine excuse? Surely you can think of something more original?' His eyes flickered over her, glimmering in the firelight. 'You're my wife now. You've no more excuses left. This time I'm going to take you, however hard you fight.'

He pulled her towards him, struggling, his fingers wrenching her hands down, her wrists aching where the cruel fingers bit into them. 'But if you fight you'll regret it, you little bitch,' he said in an ugly tone. They stared at each other. Deborah sighed, wearily, capitulating, recognising the futility of fighting him.

His hands began to move over her, exploring her with a cold determination which sent waves of misery flooding over her. She closed her eyes to escape the vision of his remorseless face, her body limp and unmoving beneath his icy caresses.

'What's the matter?' he asked, sensing her withdrawal. His voice was harsh. 'Did you enjoy it more with Robin? Perhaps I'm not making it exciting enough.' His hand brutally tilted her face. His mouth savaged her, mercilessly demanding. She kept her lips closed, sickness burning in her throat like acid. He wound his fingers in her hair, tugging back her head, trying to force her lips to open to him. 'I'll make you kiss me,' he muttered roughly. 'You may not want to, but I'll make you respond to me ...'

A tear trickled down beneath her closed lids. A sob

broke from her, muted and pathetic. She felt his body tense.

The tears ran faster, although she tried to halt them. He swore under his breath, the chilly surface of his manner breaking. 'Not tears, for God's sake,' he said bitterly. 'Not tears, you cheating little bitch!'

Shaking, she wiped a hand across her wet eyes. 'I'm sorry,' she stammered.

He swore again, then they both lay still. Her body heaved with the effort of choking back her tears. Alex suddenly pulled her against him, his hand fondling her hair, stroking it in new gentleness.

'Stop crying,' he said flatly. 'You defeat me, Deb, at every turn. I won't force you to take me.'

She sighed, her chilled limbs slowly relaxing. His kindness was like manna in a stony desert. She turned against his body, the warmth of his skin comforting. His hand moved over her hair, lifting it softly.

'This is one hell of a mess,' he said after a while. 'I should have had the decency to let you break off our marriage and marry Robin. That was what he was there for, wasn't it? To get you back?'

'He just wanted to apologise,' she said, a sigh troubling her. There was something so sweet in lying like this in his arms while he stroked her hair. She did not want to begin the barren argument again. 'Robin's fairminded. He came to say he was sorry he accused me like that.'

Alex made a sound of bitter incredulity. 'Do you think I'm fool enough to believe it? He had you in your bedroom.'

The brutality made her flinch. 'No,' she said shakily. 'That isn't true, Alex. I was sewing up his shirt—nothing else.'

Alex's hand froze on her hair. He tilted her face so that he could see it clearly, his eyes fiercely probing.

She looked back at him, the firelight flickered over her tear-stained face, but the blue eyes met his probing stare frankly.

'He made love to you,' he said disbelievingly.

'No,' she said, frightened by the hard intensity of his expression.

Alex's mouth tightened. 'He had you in a bedroom, in that damned wrap, and he never touched you?'

'He never touched me,' she said, sighing. Was the cold-eyed hostile stranger going to return?

He stared at her for a long time, his eyes flickering over her face as though he tried to penetrate behind the oval features.

After a while he asked curtly, 'But you wanted him to?'

She flushed. 'No!'

He moved restlessly, his face filled with harsh incredulity. 'I might have believed that once, Deb, but you're too passionate for me to believe it now. The ice is a very thin layer, isn't it? And the fire underneath is red-hot.'

She looked away, her lashes flickering. 'Robin has never discovered that,' she whispered, her tone an admission.

Alex breathed in sudden hoarseness. His hand turned her face round again and she looked at him in submission. The silvery eyes probed her glance until she felt a long shudder in the centre of her body. Her skin seemed to burn with heat. Alex's arms slid under her, lifting her slender body closer, and with a groan she enclosed his dark head in the circle of her embrace, meeting his kiss with a starving, abandoned response which made his lips harden into probing exploration.

He broke off the kiss, breathing hard, pulling her nightdress over her head. In the firelight she saw his eyes flicker over the white gleam of her body. 'Oh, God,

I want you,' he said deep in his throat. She looked up at him, trembling, while he tore off his own clothes, then his hands touched her, shaking, the passion of their caress totally different to the cold exploration he had offered her five minutes ago.

The erotic intimacy of his movements made her quiver in sensual response, reaching for his naked chest with an aching desire to touch him. As she touched his skin a muted whimper of satisfaction came from her. His hands were moulding her beneath him, their movements feverish and aroused, as if he needed to touch every part of her. Were his hands trembling so violently, she wondered, or was it the tension of her own hunger which made her imagine it? He had known so many other women. Jealousy wrenched at her and she gave a groan of pain.

'Did I hurt you? What is it?' he asked at once, frowning.

'This is all new to me,' she said miserably. 'There's never been anyone but you, Alex ... but all this is familiar to you. How many other women have gone crazy in your arms?'

His eyes gleamed at her admission. 'Jealousy, Deb?' For a moment she saw triumph in his face, then he smiled wryly. 'You needn't feel jealous. I don't know how other women have felt in the past, but I can tell you that I've never felt the way I feel now. Just looking at you is making me go crazy with desire, and I wouldn't want you to feel the way I felt when Robin came out of your bedroom doing up his shirt. It was like dying. I thought the pain would never stop. I wanted to scream, to kill both of you ...'

His words astounded her. 'Alex ...' Her voice held incredulity and delight. Surely such jealousy could not be anything less than love?

He made a wry face. 'Well, now you know.' He bent

his head, finding her mouth in a fierce demand, kissing her with hungry tenderness, his urgent hands caressing her until she was weak with passion, offering herself without hesitation, their bodies tangling with increasing fever. She felt light-headed, aching with the need to surrender to his possession.

The heavy masculinity of the body above her made her shudder with desire, the roughness of his thigh against the smooth skin of her own driving her mad, hardly aware that she had begun to beg him to take her, her voice muffled by his kiss.

'I've waited for this so long,' he said unsteadily into her pulsing throat. Under him her slender body arched, shuddering, as a piercing sensation of total completion swept over her, pain swamped by delight. The cosy images which had been her old idea of belonging crumbled for ever as she felt Alex merge with her own body, a shared moment of possession which brought a long, trembling cry of pleasure from her parted lips.

He paused, his breathing rapid and harsh. 'Did I hurt you? Darling, did I hurt you?'

'No, oh, no,' she whispered. Her hands pressed him down to her. 'Oh, Alex darling, I want you so much...'

He groaned, his body trembling violently. 'Deb... Oh, God, Deb, I love you like hell...' The husky words echoed in her ears as he pulled her down into a whirlpool of sensual pleasure. In that sweet turmoil, and the delight and agony of giving endlessly, Alex was utterly hers, their responses identical, drainingly intense.

She felt like the exhausted survivor of a shipwreck come safely to harbour as she lay later, entwined in his arms, stroking his hair. The warmth of the red firelight enclosed them. A great drowsiness seemed to cover them both. Alex yawned, rubbing his cheek against her.

'I could sleep for ever. I haven't slept properly since

I saw Robin at your flat.'

She pushed back the hair from his temples. 'Jealousy is agony, isn't it?' She had fought against her own jealousy for so long, but it had always defeated her, and she was glad he had felt that hellish ache too.

He turned to look up at her, his eyes veiled by their dark lashes. 'Tell me you love me, Deb,' he asked with shaky humility in his voice.

A little smile touched her mouth. She ran a finger along his mouth and he kissed it adoringly.

'Love, Alex? I thought you didn't believe in it.'

'I didn't,' he said grimly. 'You forced me to believe in it that night I saw Robin come out of your bedroom. The pain was so intense I knew I had to be suffering from more than mere sexual jealousy. I could barely speak or move. I've lost other women to new lovers, but it had never made me feel the way I felt then. It was like having a limb amputated without anaesthetic. Every breath I took hurt like hell. I could barely look at you without wanting to kill you. The thought of him ...' His voice broke off, shaking. 'Oh, God, it was agony!'

She felt the pain throbbing in his body, and she kissed him, willing him to be comforted. 'Alex darling, I love you ... I never did love Robin and he never did more than kiss me, even though he wanted you to think he had that day ...'

He held her tightly, hurting and enchanting her. 'Dearest ... oh, my dearest ...' Their mouths clung endlessly. When their lips drew reluctantly apart he sighed and stroked her cheek with a trembling hand.

'It served me right to go through that, though. I'd wanted you for years and I knew it, but I knew you had strong views about sex, and I guessed you weren't the sort of girl to go into a casual affair, so I tried to put you out of my mind. I wasn't prepared to take the way I felt about you seriously. I tried once or twice to date you, and when you refused I just shrugged my shoulders and told myself to forget it. It never really dawned on me how badly I wanted you until you said you were getting engaged to Robin. Oh, I heard, although I pretended at the time to be thinking about my trip to Stockholm. I managed to cover up the shock you'd given me, but all the time I was there I couldn't get the thought out of my head. I kept seeing you in bed with Robin.' He grimaced. 'It drove me wild. I flew back with the set intention of putting a spanner in the works. I meant to force you to be aware of me that day I came back.'

'I remember,' she said drily. 'You kissed me quite deliberately, and I suppose I knew it was planned.'

He groaned. 'It was despicable—I knew that at the time. I had no intention of marrying you then, Deb. I just knew I couldn't live with the idea of you and Robin getting married.' He curved a hand around her face, his eyes passionate.

Deborah looked at him with loving amusement. 'You were behaving with typical selfishness, Alex ...'

'I was fooling myself,' he said wryly. 'It had come home to me that if you married Robin you'd sleep with him, and the pictures that conjured up were like hot nails driven into my skull. All those months when you'd been dating Robin I'd sensed that there was no passion between the two of you. I couldn't stop watching you for signs of it, and you were as cool as two old friends. I suppose I'd always despised Robin, anyway. I knew I would have done everything in my power to get you into my bed, and it was obvious he was far too chivalrous for that, so I'd let things drift on ... until you said you were marrying him. That shook me to my foundations. I admitted to myself that I had to stop the marriage. I had to get you somehow.'

'So you invented the trip to Nice,' she said, watching his face with tenderness.

'Ricky Winter was a godsent gift,' he said wryly. 'I used him to get you out of England. I had no fixed plan in my head, except somehow to stop that damned engagement.'

'But you thought that if you turned on the heat you might manage to persuade me to give in to you,' she said drily.

'I was a swine,' he admitted apologetically.

'You very nearly succeeded,' she admitted, sighing. 'I'd fought a difficult battle against how I felt about you for years, and when you did turn on the heat I lost my head in minutes. I suppose I'd always known that if you got me into your arms I'd never have the strength to fight my way out of them again...'

His arms tightened and he groaned. 'Deb, I have to be honest. I didn't know I loved you even while we were at the cottage. I knew I wanted you badly, badly enough to offer to marry you when I failed to seduce you. I thought you were holding out for a wedding ring, that that was the price you set on coming to bed with me, and I felt very resentful when I said I'd marry you.'

'I knew that,' she said, remembering her own hurt with a sigh. 'Had you told me that night that you loved me I would have slept with you, though, Alex.'

He groaned again. 'I nearly blew a blood vessel when you refused me, you know. I thought you must have egged me on to make a fool of myself so that you could have the amusement of knowing I'd been that crazy to get you...'

'I realised that,' she said, wincing at the memory of his savage hatred as he stalked out of the room.

'I had visions of the joke going around London, of my friends smiling behind their hands at the thought of my proposing marriage and still failing to get you into bed ... you were right when you said I'd been fooled by my own image. My machismo got badly punctured that night. God, I was angry with you! I had used every trick in the book, and you'd beaten me hands down. I told myself I hated you.'

'You told me that, too,' she smiled, tongue in cheek.

'I meant it, too,' he said roughly. 'When we got stuck at the cottage I told myself I couldn't care less about you, but I had this secret feeling of relief because I thought I'd prevented your engagement after all. I thought Robin must suspect I'd slept with you, and I knew that any man's pride would be stung by your absence on such a thin excuse. I sniped at you because I wanted to get reactions from you. Every time you came near me I was confused ... I wanted to hurt you, to touch you ... I couldn't make sense of my own feelings any more. I'd never felt anything like it in my life. But I couldn't recognise it as love, because I just didn't believe in it, so I thought it was an intense sexual need which your refusal had frustrated to the point of real pain.'

She stroked his hard cheek with one hand, watching his eyes flare with confused emotion. Alex looked at her, his bones tensing beneath her fingers.

'That day in the garden,' he said huskily, 'I wanted you so badly I was shaking ...'

'I know,' she said tenderly. 'I felt the same. At that moment nothing mattered but to give myself to you, even though I knew you didn't love me the way I loved you.'

He made a low sound and kissed her, his mouth fiercely demanding. 'Oh, God, that was when I began to think you might love me,' he said thickly. 'Until then I'd just thought you wanted me but wanted me to go through the motions of being in love to satisfy your sense of morality. I knew I affected you. I could feel it when I touched you. But you held me off and I thought it was for Robin's sake at first, then I told myself it was just a hypocritical desire to be virtuous. Then you looked at me so lovingly when you submitted that I felt my heart shake.'

'Oh, darling,' she muttered, pressing against him.

He kissed the top of her head. 'That was when it occurred to me that I wouldn't mind being married to you ...'

She gave a soft little laugh at his tone. 'Oh, you really can be a patronising devil, Alex!'

He smiled, acknowledging the truth. 'It was my usual selfishness, I know. I started to tell myself that it was the only way I'd ever get you, that it would be fun anyway ... and it would put a stop for ever to the chance of any other man having you ...'

Her eyes were filled with wry laughter. 'Oh, Alex!'

'Darling, I was kidding myself,' he said, grimacing. 'I was wildly looking for excuses for doing what I knew I wanted badly to do by then. When Robin insulted you it gave me the chance to say I was going to marry you. I couldn't bring myself to propose to you again and have you turn me down, but I knew damned well it was because by then I had to know you were mine.'

She turned bonelessly in his arms, her face radiant. 'Oh, Alex, I love you!'

He held her so tightly she could scarcely breathe and it was a pain which was sheer delight. 'Even knowing as I did that I wanted to marry you badly I couldn't bring myself to admit I was in love. It wasn't until I walked into your flat and saw Robin that the truth burst on me. I had refused to believe in my feelings for you except as a desirable woman. I had to believe in the agony I felt then. I don't know how to describe how I felt. I couldn't move or speak because of pain. It wasn't just sexual jealousy. It was because I thought you must prefer him to me after all or you would never have gone to bed with him. I knew you too well to think you would have done it casually. I thought Robin had wanted you to prove you were still innocent, and you'd done it because you loved him ...'

She flushed, then looked at him incredulously. 'Yet you still forced me to marry you?' Her tone was disbelieving.

Alex flushed darkly. 'I told you I was a swine. I was so jealous, so bitter, I wanted to kill both of you. If I'd been a nicer man I might have walked out of your flat and walked under a bus. The way I felt it was what I would have done. But I didn't. I was so unused to love I stayed, and I forced you to marry me, not because I couldn't let you go ... but because I was still such a selfish, egotistical swine that I was prepared to ruin your life to stop another man having you.'

She looked at him wryly. 'That's quite an admission from you, Alex.'

'You've made me face a lot of facts about myself, Deb. I don't like what I've seen, but I know they're all true. I was surprised you didn't put up a harder fight against me, but I was still cynical about women, so I thought you must realise what a much better match I am than Robin. I was convinced you loved him, and I was very bitter. When we came to bed tonight I fully intended to possess you even if you fought like hell.'

'That was obvious,' she said, remembering with a shudder.

'I was like a madman,' he said in anguish. 'I kept thinking about you in Robin's arms, and that you had resisted me all along but let him have you ... and I wanted to hurt you as savagely as you'd hurt me. I never want to feel that sort of jealousy again.' He sighed, a long hard sigh. 'When you started to cry I seemed to come out of a trance of bitter madness. I realised I couldn't hurt you like that. I felt sick. I thought you wanted Robin and I almost cried myself.'

'Don't look like that, Alex,' she begged, wrung by the pain in his lean face.

His lips moved over her face, pressing hotly against her temples, eyes, cheeks. 'You don't know how I felt as I faced the thought that I'd have to let you go back to him. I told myself I'd have to get the marriage annulled and let Robin have you after all, and that was the moment I hit rock bottom. You cried in my arms, and I lay there, unable to fight the way I felt any more, enduring hell ...'

'Don't!' she whispered, moved by his words.

'When you swore he had never touched you I couldn't let myself believe it at first. It was like being shown a glimpse of heaven after one has fallen into damnation. I'd always believed sex was all that could attract a man to a woman, but when you looked at me so tenderly and I began to hope you loved me instead of Robin, it had nothing to do with sex. It was a totally new feeling. I've always been pretty arrogant in my affairs with women. At that moment I could have gone on my knees to you.' His hands framed her face and he looked at her with deep, passionate adoration. 'You said you were jealous of the other women I've known, darling. You needn't be. Every emotion I've ever felt was a pale shadow of what you've made me go through. None of them ever drove me insane with desire, as you have, or made me suffer agonies or feel totally humble, as you have. There will never be anyone else, I swear to you. After you refused me at Nice there was one point when I told myself I'd bring you to your knees ... instead you brought me to mine, and I knew everything else in life but you was meaningless to me.'

'I reached that point when I almost surrendered to you in my room at Nice,' she said, sighing. 'I knew very well I was sexually aware of you, but I knew all about the other women who had felt your compelling charm ...' Her blue eyes mocked him. 'I wasn't joining any queues. I hated the way you made me feel, until you made me admit I wanted you, out on that raft.'

His silvery eyes narrowed teasingly. 'You've no idea what that did to my blood pressure. It shot sky-high, Deb. You were like a different woman. I was astonished and delighted by the way you took fire ...'

She blushed. 'You vain, egotistical devil ... you and your damned silver medallion! I could feel it against me as you made me face the way I wanted you ...'

Mocking amusement filled his face. 'Ah, Sammy,' he said softly.

The old jealousy pierced her and she looked at him in pain.

Alex laughed, eyes warm. 'Darling, Sammy and I were never lovers. It was all a publicity stunt. Sammy's a nice girl. She knew it was a game and she was no more interested in me than I was in her.'

Deborah's eyes widened. She saw from his face that he told the truth.

'Half the time my so-called affairs were sheer moonshine. I thought you realised that. It was a convenient way of getting free publicity, but I'm not the sexual athlete the gossip columnists see me as, darling. Oh, once or twice, it was more concrete. I'm not saying there were no women, but the sexy image was useful to me, that was all.'

'Your mother said that,' she murmured.

'You said it, too,' he reminded her. 'You told me I was beginning to believe my own publicity. I hated to admit it, but you were right. Even when you snapped the chain of Sammy's medallion, and I wondered if you were jealous of the women I'd known, I was such a conceited idiot that I was pleased at the thought. It showed you were by no means as indifferent as you wanted me to believe...'

'I wasn't indifferent, damn you,' she said, stung by the brightness of his eyes. 'Once I admitted to myself I wanted you I knew I loved you. I'd never wanted a man like that before. The nagging ache you made me feel was new to me. Unlike you I'd never felt the urge for sex without love...'

'God help you if you ever do,' he said, his voice thick, his hands hard as they held her. 'I think I'd kill you!'

She looked at him through her lashes, seeing cruelty in his face with a leap of the senses. 'I never will,' she promised softly. 'I wanted to give you my body only because you already had my heart.' The hands grew possessive, caressing her body with trembling gentleness. 'You could have taken me in the garden,' she said, shakily. 'I was at your mercy, Alex, even though I knew you didn't love me.'

'Why did you refuse to marry me that first time?' he asked, staring at her.

'Because I knew you didn't love me, and I couldn't have borne it,' she admitted. 'It hurt to say no, but I wanted your love, not just your lovemaking.'

'I knew that tonight when you cried and I realised I couldn't take you knowing you didn't love me,' he said sombrely. 'I knew then that sex without love was as bitter as gall.'

Deborah moaned. 'But love makes you so weak. When you made love to me in the garden I had lost the strength to refuse you. I knew I was going to let you, even though it would scar me for life, because I loved you so desperately.'

'Darling,' he muttered, the hard, experienced hands shaking as he held her. 'Oh, darling, I nearly died of frustration when my mother arrived ... but tonight made up for everything. I thought I knew everything there was to know about sex, but tonight you gave me the most intense pleasure I've ever had in my life ...'

'I love you,' she said, her voice quivering with happiness. 'Alex, I love you.'

He gave a long groan of hard, hoarse pleasure. 'Deb ... Oh, God, Deb, I want you ...'

Deborah began to laugh at the familiar phrase from which she had shrunk so many times, but her laughter died as Alex rolled her towards him and passionately silenced her.

Mills & Boon

PUT MORE ROMANCE INTO CHRISTMAS

CAMPAIGN FOR LOVING
Penny Jordan

DANGEROUS STUNT
Mary Lyons

LINKED FROM THE PAST
Mary Wibberley

A PAST REVENGE
Carole Mortimer

Give the gift of romance this Christmas – four brand new titles from Mills & Boon, attractively gift wrapped for £4.40.

Make this a romantic Christmas. Look for this gift pack where you buy Mills & Boon romances.

Available from 12th October 1984.